MW00533066

THE AMISH COWBOY'S MAKEOVER

AMISH COWBOYS OF MONTANA
BOOK V

ADINA SENFT

Copyright 2023 Shelley Adina Senft Bates

No part of this publication may be reproduced, distributed or transmitted in
any form or by any means, including photocopying, recording, or other
electronic or mechanical methods, without the prior written permission of
the publisher, except in the case of brief quotations embodied in critical
reviews and certain other noncommercial uses permitted by copyright law.
For permission requests, write to the publisher at www.moonshellbooks.com.

This is a work of fiction. Names, characters, places, and incidents are a
product of the author's imagination. Locales and public names are sometimes
used for atmospheric purposes. Any resemblance to actual people, living or
dead, or to businesses, companies, events, institutions, or locales is
completely coincidental.

Cover design by Carpe Librum Book Design. Images used under license. *"Er
hat ein Weib genommen"* translated by Shelley Adina Senft Bates.

The Amish Cowboy's Makeover / Adina Senft—1st ed.

ISBN 978-1-950854-79-0 R080123

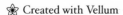 Created with Vellum

PRAISE FOR ADINA SENFT

"Filled with spiritual insights and multilayered story-lines. At times readers will be chuckling and other times, misty eyed as the book unfolds."

— AMISH READER ON *HERB OF GRACE*

"The first thing I loved about this story from Adina Senft is that it's set in Montana—we don't get many Amish stories set on the Western side of the US, so it was fun to shift gears from farming to ranching. The Montana landscape in winter is an added bonus! I also loved that this is a prequel to her Montana Millers series, the origin story, if you will, of the Circle M Ranch and the love story that accompanies it. This story is a girl-next-door romance with layered characters and an overall sweetness to the tone that warms the heart."

— CARRIE SCHMIDT, READING IS MY SUPERPOWER, ON *THE AMISH COWBOY'S CHRISTMAS*

"Adina Senft has once again produced a simply sweet and engaging Amish romance novel, filled with twists and turns, enjoyable beyond compare."

— AMISH READER ON *BALM OF GILEAD*

Grateful thanks to horsewoman and fellow chicken lover
Judi Fleming.
Thanks as well to my husband, who got caught up in auction fever and
won the bidding on the "Earth and Stars" quilt just for me.

THE AMISH COWBOY'S
MAKEOVER

MOUNTAIN HOME, MONTANA

Second week of August

FROM THE DOORWAY of his smithy, Alden Stolzfus saw Malena Miller tie up her horse in front of Rose Garden Quilts, his mother's fabric and quilt store. Mamm was somewhere inside getting organized for the day before she unlocked the door, but here was Malena, standing by the horse's head and looking as though she was giving serious thought to untying the rein and driving away.

Alden was not about to let that happen. Chances to speak to her alone didn't come along very often. So, though he had some serious work to do for the Rocking Diamond if their fancy front gates were to be ready by Friday, he removed his leather apron, settled his straw hat on his head, and ambled across Main Street trying not to look like he was in a hurry to reach her.

"*Guder mariye*, Malena," he said when he was within hailing distance.

She didn't jump, but her hand tightened on the horse's bridle, making the animal sidestep nervously before they both regained their composure.

"*Guder mariye*, Alden," she replied, giving him the smile she offered to everyone on a church Sunday, or at a get-together of the *Youngie*, or in a casual meeting like this. Even if it wasn't one of her special smiles that could light up a room, it still had plenty of candle power. It was enough to nearly make him forget how to talk.

"I'm waiting for your *mamm* to open," she said unnecessarily. "She's inside?"

"Oh, *ja*," he said. "She likes to take a little time to get organized before the day starts." He tried not to peer into the open buggy, where two big plastic bags lay on the passenger seat.

Malena seemed to feel she owed him an explanation. "I brought a couple of my quilts, hoping she might take them on consignment." Color flooded her cheeks. "I suppose every quilter in the Siksika Valley comes here, hoping for the same thing."

Even if they did, his mother was no fool. Malena's quilts would sell faster than the hotcakes over at the Bitterroot Dutch Café. When he said as much, she blushed even deeper, as though he'd been making fun.

"You're just saying that to be nice," she said.

"I'm saying it because it's true. Your quilts are the next best thing to art. Not that I know anything about art. But I've seen some of what goes into a quilt."

She didn't look convinced.

"How can anyone as talented as you think so little of her ability?" he blurted, forgetting to be tactful in his desire to be honest.

A crinkle formed between reddish brows blessed with an arch like a butterfly's feelers. "Because I don't want to be *hochmut* about it, and displease *der Herr*, like Bishop Joe says."

"You're the last person I would say suffered from *hochmut*." Pride was a sin in Amish eyes, and he had never seen her show symptoms of it. Especially when it came to her talent. That was the candle most definitely hidden under the bushel basket, with probably some metaphorical boards and an old saddle thrown on top for good measure.

He couldn't understand it. She was the life of every get-together, the girl with the teasing comeback to every line, the one who threw back her head and laughed when something tickled her funny bone. She was like a fire in a fireplace, brightening any room and lending warmth to everyone in it. If she was absent from one of the frolics the *Youngie* enjoyed, some zest went out of it, and he'd find himself wanting to go home early, much to the dismay of his younger sisters, who rode with him.

He opened his mouth to speak, but the door of Rose Garden Quilts rattled and Mamm swung open the door to greet the August morning.

"Hallo, Malena," she said in surprise, with the smile everyone seemed unable to prevent whenever they saw her. "You're in town early."

"*Ja.*" Malena's throat closed, and she tried again. "I was hoping to talk with you, if you had a minute."

"I have several minutes." Mamm stood aside to let Malena into the shop, while Alden took the soft, bulky bags from the buggy and carried them in. "At nine o'clock on a Tuesday morning, unless the bus arrives packed with quilters, business won't pick up until the breakfast crowd comes out of the café."

Alden leaned down to prop the door open with a bit of ironwork he'd made of a climbing rose. It was heavy enough to hold the door, yet looked at home in a shop bursting with color and design. All along the street, he'd made iron sign holders for many of the shop owners. They stuck out above the doors, swinging signs hanging from them the way he'd seen in pictures of the Old West. Mamm's carved wooden sign had a matching climbing rose.

"*Denki*, Alden," Mamm said, and she went to join Malena.

There was nothing for it but to return to his order for the Rocking Diamond. Alden's wagon waited in the small barn at the rear of the smithy with its slats down, custom-built inside to enable him to be a mobile farrier. He'd apprenticed to the farrier in Shipshewana, where he'd grown up, and taken up smithing with his father when they'd moved to St Ignatius. When Dat had met up with that bull—the one thing stronger and more ornery than he—the smithy had become Alden's, young as he'd been. After the funeral, Mamm had acted on an invitation from her Yoder cousins here in Mountain Home and moved up to the Siksika.

Here, Alden felt like he'd really come home. The Yoders had helped him prepare his shop, which had once been an outbuilding next to Yoder's Variety Store, after they'd seen Mamm settled in a tiny house in town. And when her fabric and quilts had needed more space, *Gott* had seen to it that a retail space came available right across the street, which was also the highway through town. That meant that tourists were tempted to stop, and using the brains *der Herr* had given him, he'd soon learned to augment practical things like horseshoes and cattle gates with kitchen things like paper towel spindles and racks for bath towels, which he could sell in the variety store.

In the distance, where the highway formed a kind of Z, the middle part being Mountain Home's downtown, he heard the sound of a powerful engine. He had enough time to get back across the road before it arrived. Big trucks were rare on this county highway, which carried mostly Amish buggies and farm pickups and flatbeds. Alden had just crossed the yellow line when with a roar, a tricked-out pickup truck with about an acre of chrome, fog lamps, and a comealong on a big rack on the grill appeared like magic.

With a screech of brakes and a horn that sounded like Gabriel's trumpet having a bad day, the truck rocked to a stop practically on Alden's heels as he gained the wooden sidewalk. The passenger window slid down soundlessly.

"You aiming to get yourself killed?" A man about his own age leaned over, his left arm draped over the wheel. "I almost hit you."

"Speed limit's twenty-five in town," Alden said mildly, stepping up beside the door. "Lot of buggies and horses on the roads. You'll want to be careful."

"Buggies, like in *Gunsmoke?*" The stranger looked interested.

Alden had no idea what that was. "Buggies, like in Amish." He nodded toward Malena's open two-seater, the chestnut mare waiting patiently at the rail.

"Oh." The interest faded. "Say, you couldn't direct me to a ranch around here, could you? It's called the Rocking Diamond."

"Sure." He eyed the driver. Hair cut short with a wave in the front. A tanned face, with vivid blue eyes that reminded Alden of lightning about to strike. Beside him on the passenger seat, a brand new granite-gray Resistol hat rested wrong way up. "You visiting the Madisons? Kind of late in the year to be signing on as a hand." Though he'd probably be welcome. Any extra pair of hands was, at this time of year. And with this truck, he'd fit right in. Trey Madison had one similar.

The young man shook his head. "I suppose a hand is what you'd call me. So, directions?"

Alden pointed west, and told him how to get there. With a wave of thanks, the young man spun the wheel and the truck pulled away. His ability to do the speed limit lasted until the second turn in the road. Alden heard him gun the engine as the highway straightened out on its journey through the valley and there was that roar again, fading into the distance.

Shaking his head, he returned to the forge. It was a good thing the county had shown its appreciation for what the Amish community had done for the tourist trade, and resurfaced the roads with shoulders that were good and wide. He sent up a prayer that both animals and humans would survive the truck's five-mile flight across country.

MALENA CHEWED ON THE INSIDE OF HER CHEEK AS SHE waited for Rose Stolzfus's verdict. If the young widow had been a judge at the county fair, Malena couldn't have been more nervous. When Alden had compared her quilts to art a little while ago, it had been difficult not to confide that he was more accurate than he knew. For what was art but something that came out of a person—that had been put there in the first place by God? How could she take credit for that, as though she'd had anything to do with it?

She'd been making patterns out of fabric ever since she could remember, making bed covers for her faceless dolls and then graduating to place mats for the Miller table. The first time Mamm had allowed her and Rebecca to stay inside and join the ladies at a quilting frolic had been a revelation. Something had opened up inside her, not unlike the joy of meeting an old friend. After that, the county library had a hard time keeping the quilt books on the shelves. She'd read every single one, making notes and diagrams. Finally the head librarian had taken to sending a note home when she saw one of the Millers in town, to let Malena know they had a new book in. Quilting frolics had become something to look forward to, and then something she could organize, and finally she was allowed to help in the quilt tent at the annual auction to benefit their little one-room school.

Rose shook out her Glacier Lily quilt over the big square box that was meant to look like a bed, built so people could see their prospective purchase and imagine it in their home. The display had already been made up with another Amish woman's quilt, but Rose snapped the Glacier Lily out over it and let it settle into shape.

Then she gazed at it silently until Malena thought she might chew her way right through her own cheek. The yellow glacier lily was her favorite flower—the first real flower of spring in Montana. She'd appliquéd a three-foot wreath of them in the center of the quilt and then used muted greens, blues, and cream in a block of her own design she called the Montana Star behind the wreath.

"How's the quilt auction coming along?"

Malena's anxiety climbed. Did Rose mean she wouldn't sell the Glacier Lily here? That she ought to put it up for auction?

Rose glanced at her. "Sadie's in charge this year, ain't so?"

The bishop's wife, the most shy woman in the valley, had

only been prodded into it because Aendi Annie King wasn't well enough for the job anymore. "She is, but Ruby and I are her hands and feet. And her nose, as my brother Zach will be the first to tell you."

"An organizer's nose has to be into everything if she's going to do it properly," Rose told her with an air of experience. "How many entries do you have?"

"Not as many as we'd hoped," Malena confessed. "Around twenty so far. But we're hoping for a couple from Holmes County, and at least one from Lancaster County. We've discovered that changing the date from May to August might not have been such a *gut* idea."

"Why not?"

"We thought we would attract tourists before the *Englisch Kinner* start school. Last winter, when we were talking about it, we thought we could handle it as well as harvest and canning and roundup. We were ... too optimistic. On top of that, the quilters who might have sent things in May sent them to the Rexford and St Ignatius school auctions instead."

"Ah. In June and July."

Malena nodded. "But people will still come, I'm sure of it. Who wouldn't want to stop in the Siksika to enjoy an auction and some *gut* Amish cooking before going on to Glacier National Park?" She took a deep breath as Rose shook out the second quilt, a traditional Amish nine-patch diamond set on point in the middle, with bands of color in a square around it, held in place by black squares. Its colors were those found in their district's clothes—black, green, burgundy, purple, blue, even a few discreet strips of yellow and rose pink. A plain quilt, to be sure, until you looked closely and saw the whorls of the feathers that Malena had designed for it. It had taken the

Miller women hours upon hours during winter evenings, and gave the quilt its true beauty.

"If the committee had put these quilts on the advertising brochure, Malena, you wouldn't have had to worry," Rose said.

It took a moment to understand what she meant. "Do you ... like them?"

"*Like* them." Rose was a guarded sort of person. Malena had learned she didn't make friends easily, despite how pretty she was. But now she slipped an arm around Malena's shoulders and squeezed. "I love them. I want them for myself, and that is a very slippery slope for a quilt shop owner." She released her and gave a sudden gleam of a smile. "I could put a price tag of a thousand dollars on each one of these this morning and someone would hand it over by the weekend."

Malena's breath went out of her in a rush. *"What?"*

"Not a word of exaggeration. If you put the Glacier Lily up for auction next weekend, you'd get more than that. I'd estimate fifteen hundred."

"That's impossible." Malena was having a hard time getting words out. Or breathing.

"If betting weren't a sin, I'd bet you one of the café's cupcakes that you're wrong. So here's what I'm going to do." Rose went around behind the counter. "I'll take the Amish Diamond for the shop. It will go in the window and help bring attention to the advertisement for the school auction. We split the asking price sixty-forty, which I do for all the quilters."

"Forty percent for me?" Malena had not expected so much.

"No, sixty percent for you."

How could *der Herr* rain so many blessings on a person, all in one morning? Malena didn't know what to say.

Kindly overlooking Malena's mouth opening and closing

like a trout landed on a creek bank, Rose went on, "Enter the Glacier Lily in the auction. It's for the valley's *Kinner*. I can't think of a better cause for this beautiful quilt."

Malena didn't so much make up her mind as release the words that *Gott* put in her mouth. "All right," she said. "I will."

As Mamm might say, Malena hardly knew whether she was coming or going. Luckily, Hester knew the way back to the Circle M Ranch better than anybody—certainly better than she did right now.

Fifteen hundred dollars for the Glacier Lily! Malena had never seen that much money in her life. Mind you, she wouldn't see what the quilt fetched, either, for all the money was going to the school fund for repairs and maintenance, some desks, new textbooks and workbooks, and a couple of cords of cut and stacked firewood for the woodstove that kept the scholars warm during the bright, frigid days of a Montana winter.

But just the fact that Rose, who was the closest Malena knew to an authority about quilt prices, thought the Glacier Lily would fetch such a sum was a balm to her soul. She didn't suffer from false modesty—*der Herr* had given her a gift, and she did her best to glorify Him by creating the beauty He put in her head. And money didn't give a quilt its value, not really. Value was in the eyes of a woman like Rose as she gazed at a quilt, took it into her soul, and loved it. Wanted to have it in her home, to give her joy. That was where its value lay.

But *believing* that a man or woman could feel that way about her work? That was the creek Malena had a hard time jumping. She loved her quilts, but as her brother Zach had once told her as he closed his sketchbook on some wonderful drawing, "It never looks as good as it does in my head."

Maybe that was a gift from God, too. Just to keep a person humble.

Hester's pace picked up as they passed the three-mile marker that denoted the boundary line of the Bontrager place. One driveway and a couple of gates, and the four-mile marker would tell her she was at the corner of the Circle M's eastern-most paddock, and home.

Just as she rounded the curve, Hester whickered and came to a clattering stop at the sight of a great big pickup nose down in a broad ditch full of Queen Anne's Lace. A man waved at her as he slid out the passenger side and rammed a gray cowboy hat on his head.

"Glad to see someone at last," he called as he loped through the flowers and climbed the slope toward them. "Is the highway always this deserted?"

"*Neh*—I mean, no," she said. "It's Tuesday. People have already gone to work if they're going to, but usually there are lots of tourists."

He reached the shoulder of the road and extended a hand to pat Hester's neck.

The horse was used to people, but even so, she sidestepped and tossed her head.

He grinned as he looked up at her, and Malena blinked. How was it possible for anybody to be this good looking? His cheekbones could cut glass, his mouth was mobile and full, and his eyes, my goodness! They took her in with a frank appraisal that warmed into admiration. The breeze touched the back of her neck, exposed where her untameable red hair was pinned up under her white *Kapp*, and raised goosebumps.

Gracious. To break the spell, she said, "Something happen to your truck?"

Hands on hips, he turned away to survey the shiny truck nose deep in flowers. "Yeah. A deer. At least, I think it was. Could have been an elk. I tried to avoid it and wound up like that. Guess I should have listened to the guy in town."

"What guy?"

He shrugged one shoulder, which only served to make her notice that his chambray shirt sleeves were rolled up, and those arms looked as though tossing hay bales wouldn't be a problem for him. "An Amish guy. Young. Straw hat. Told me I was speeding."

That pretty much described half the men in the Siksika Valley. She shrugged it aside. "Where were you heading?"

"The Rocking Diamond."

"That's not far. A couple of miles, on the other side of our place." She waved a hand toward the grassy acres on the opposite side of the road.

"A couple of miles may not be far to you, but these boots weren't made for walking." He waggled one foot to show her some pointy-toed bit of silver-trimmed nonsense no self-respecting cowboy would put on his feet. "I don't suppose you could give me a ride? I'm going to need some help getting my truck back on the road. I don't think it's damaged. But there's a lot of water down there."

"It is a ditch."

"I see that, smarty. What's your name?"

"Malena."

"Ma-lay-na." He said her name as though he were calling her. "Pretty. I'm Cord McLean."

The name rang a bell, but she didn't know why. "Well, hop in, Cord McLean. Trey and Chance Madison will get you out of there. Too bad you didn't spin and go in rear end first. That comealong won't do much good where it is."

"Now you tell me," he grumbled. He climbed into the buggy with the ease of someone who had done it a thousand times. Which was odd, considering his footwear. But she wasn't about to remark on it.

Instead, she shook the reins over Hester's back and guided her around the protruding bed of the truck. "Have you hired on at the Rocking Diamond?"

"That's what the other guy asked, too. I'll tell you what I told him. In a way. I'm going to be training there."

"Oh?" The Rocking Diamond was a very expensive dude ranch. "Are you going to learn to ride a horse?"

He laughed as though she had told him a joke. "I want to learn the whole shebang. Riding, roping, cattle, you name it. By the end of the month, I aim to be a cowboy."

Now it was her turn to laugh. "By the end of the year, maybe. Or ten. I've lived here all my life and I'm still learning."

"You're a cowpoke?"

Why did it feel like he was taking up three-quarters of the seat? He wasn't—the Glacier Lily in its bag rested between them—but it felt like it. "No, but my four brothers are. Hester, *neh*, we're not going home yet."

The horse had drifted to the left to make the turn into their lane, and Malena guided her back, much to her confusion. Cord McLean took in the sign hanging from the crossbeam held up by two stout posts. "The Circle M, huh? What's the M stand for?"

"Our last name. Miller."

"And you're Amish. I've never met an Amish person in my life, and now I've met two within an hour. Plus an Amish horse."

"You'll probably meet more," she told him. "There are more than twenty families in the Siksika Valley. Mostly ranchers, but many provide services. Like the variety store in town. The blacksmith. The quilt shop."

"And you?" he said, gazing at her, though anyone else would have been gazing at the scenery. "What do you do?"

"I'm a quilter."

"Is that a thing?"

"If you mean, is that a way to make a living, I don't know. It's just what I do. Along with helping my mother with the babies and the house, and looking after the animals, and doing ranch work, and weeding the garden, and canning vegetables, and making pickles and pies and three meals a day, and—"

"Whoa!" He held up his hands, laughing. "I'm getting tired just listening." He waited. "Aren't you going to ask me what I do?"

She shrugged. He was *Englisch*. It could be anything. Or nothing.

"See now, I like that about you. You're giving me my privacy. It's a rare thing. Thank you, Malena Miller."

She was doing no such thing, but there wasn't much point in correcting him. They were nearly at the crossroads and the Rocking Diamond's drive.

She pointed. "See those two pines, taller than the others? That's the Rocking Diamond's property line. And that building on the other side, past the stop sign, is our school."

He peered through the trees. "It looks like a cabin."

"A bit bigger. But it fits all eight grades and a couple of teachers, too."

"Eight grades in a one-room schoolhouse?" He looked delighted. "For real?"

"That's normal for us," she told him. "Probably not for you, though."

"You got that right. My high school graduating class was four hundred."

There weren't that many *Youngie* in the whole county. "We don't go to high school. After eighth grade, we go to work. The boys apprentice, usually. Girls work at home."

"Making pickles and pies and all that."

She nodded, and guided Hester into the left turn. At the closed gates, when he didn't move, she said, "Here we are."

"The Rocking Diamond?" He looked from the gates to her. "Aren't we going in?"

"You can. I need to get home. I have work to do." Dat got along just fine with the Madisons, and so did her eldest brother Daniel, but after Taylor Madison's little stunt trying to buy Joshua's fiancée's hay farm out from under her, the less Malena had to do with them, the better.

"How far is it to the house?"

Those silly boots must be more uncomfortable even than they looked. "Half a mile or so. Can you make it?"

"Of course." Those intense blue eyes settled on her. "I just thought that, being neighbors, you might take me up there and introduce me."

She nearly laughed at the thought of this forward young man needing help with an introduction. Instead, she rolled her eyes with only a little exaggeration. "Fine. Get the gate, then, and I'll drive you up."

He hopped out and opened the gate, then when she drove through and stopped, got in again.

Hester did not move. Neither did Malena.

After a moment, he said, "What? Why are we sitting here?"

"The first thing to learn about being a cowboy is the Law of the Gate."

"Which is?"

"Leave it like you found it," she told him. "If it's open, leave it open. If it's closed—"

"Close it. All right. So? I did my part. There's nothing stopping you from closing it."

Oh, did he have a lot to learn. "Driver manages the horse. Or the truck, on this place. Passenger gets the gate."

"Fine." He climbed down again, and with rather more care than it deserved, closed the gate and dropped the bar into place. "Happy now?"

"Don't ask me. Ask Brock Madison when his cattle get out on the highway because they busted down a fence and this was the only gate between them and Canada."

He didn't say another word all the way up the drive. When the house came into view, he straightened on the seat. "Nice."

To Malena, the Madison house looked more like a hotel than a home. It was enormous. Josh said it was five thousand square feet and had eight bathrooms, but she'd never been inside to count them. Granted, people paid ten thousand dollars a week to stay there, so maybe they wanted their own bathrooms. But imagine cleaning that much house.

As she pulled Hester to a halt in the wide circular sweep, Trey and his mother, Taylor Madison, came out on the deck. "Good heavens," she heard Mrs Madison say as she descended the flagstone steps. "Is that one of the Miller girls?"

Cord got out of the buggy.

"Mrs Madison," Malena said politely, "this is Cord McLean. He ran off the road and needs some help getting his truck out of the ditch. It's at the four-mile marker."

As though someone had turned up a lamp inside her, Taylor Madison glowed into a broad smile. "Mr McLean, this is a fine welcome for you. But I'm so glad you've arrived safely." She glanced at Malena. "Thank you, um ..."

"This is Malena Miller," Cord said with a grin that matched that of his new boss's wife. "She saved my life. Or at least my feet."

Mrs Madison inspected his boots, her plucked eyebrows raised. "I see. I hope you have another pair. If not, we can find something for you. After we get your truck out of the ditch. This is my eldest son, Trey. He'll give you a hand."

"Nice to meet you," Trey said easily. "Come on. Truck's in the garage."

Since Cord didn't seem to need her anymore, Malena gave a wave good-bye that nobody saw, shook the reins over Hester's back, and guided the buggy around the sweep. She set a smart pace back down the drive, and a good thing, too. She'd barely made the right turn onto the shoulder of the highway when Trey's big red pickup wheeled around the corner and passed her with a honk of its horn that could have meant *thanks* or *good-bye* or *get out of the way*. Cord waved out the passenger window and in the next moment, they were around the bend and out of sight.

A bird trilled overhead, and two crows started an argument, one in each of the pines that marked the edge of the dude ranch's property. Hester's hooves made a familiar clip-clop on the asphalt, and the breeze carried the scent of the bishop's hay field, which he'd cut yesterday.

Malena loved that smell. Not only its sweetness. Cut hay

meant cows that could be fed on dark winter days, and fed cows meant healthy calves in early spring, and healthy calves brought in money. With ranch work, one thing led into another, and everything tied together. Sure, there were disasters like frozen water pumps and coyotes and dry springs. But on the whole, it was a rewarding life, its neverending work the best way she knew to stay close to the land and serve *der Herr* who had made it.

She hoped the new hand at the Rocking Diamond would learn to appreciate it. Between those boots and his truck, though, it seemed he had a long way to go.

$\mathscr{H}$ 3 $\mathscr{H}$

AT TWENTY-FOUR YEARS OF AGE, Alden no longer thought of Beth and Julie as his *little* sisters. At twenty-one and twenty-two, they had been running around for five years already, though he wouldn't really call it that. He couldn't imagine Beth trying to smoke a cigarette, or Julie hiding a pair of jeans in the shed behind their little home. For them, *Rumspringe* was more along the lines of a trip to Whitefish on the train after spring breakup take the ski lift up and hike back down with a large group of the *Youngie*. In winter, they'd help their Yoder cousins bank up snow to create a rectangular hockey rink, and fill it with water that would freeze solid for games.

Julie's slap shot was something you remembered for a week if you were unlucky enough to get in the way.

His sisters looked after their home and picked up outside work where they could. Every day he and Mamm closed their respective shops and went home for lunch. It was a walk of only two blocks, and the girls would have hot food ready when they came in. Today Alden was racking his brain for a way to find out why Malena had wanted to speak to Mamm this morning, without looking like he wanted to know.

To his relief, Mamm brought it up herself. Alden savored his hot macaroni and cheese, cold ham slices, tomato salad, and pickled beans while his curiosity was satisfied.

"I think she can get fifteen hundred dollars for that quilt at the auction," Mamm said.

A piece of ham went down sideways and Alden coughed. He grabbed his glass of water while Julie said, "I've heard Rexford can get prices like that from some of the really good quilters back east. But Malena's quilt?"

"It must be really something," Beth said. "I can't wait to see it. Alden, are you all right?"

He nodded, and finally managed to speak. "That's an awful lot of money."

"It's an awfully beautiful quilt," Mamm said. "I hope whoever wins the bidding on it realizes what they have, and appreciates it."

If Alden had ever toyed with the notion of buying one of Malena's quilts simply for the joy of being able to touch something she had envisioned and created, it evaporated now. Fifteen hundred was more than he sometimes made in a week.

"Are all quilts that expensive?" He'd never been in the quilt tent to see them auctioned off. Instead, he'd be out in the field, perusing the stacks of used metals and parts for his business, or making cautious bids on vintage tools that ran on elbow grease, not electricity.

"*Neh*," Beth said. "They usually fetch about four hundred for the smaller ones to eight or nine hundred for a queen size. But the really beautiful ones—" She grinned with a memory. "Last year Julie and I were helping to put the quilts up for bid on the clothesline they use to display them. Remember that *Englisch* lady?"

Julie laughed. "She was so mad that this other lady was bidding against her she ran right up to the front. I thought she was going to grab it off the line. The auctioneer had to stop the bidding and convince her to sit down."

It was a good thing he wouldn't be anywhere near the quilt tent when Malena's quilt came up for bid. He could just see himself throwing his body in front of it to prevent its new owner from taking it away.

Time to change the subject to something less personal.

"I nearly got run over by an *Englisch* guy this morning when I left the shop," he said, helping himself to more bean pickles. "Driving a big tricked-out pickup. I told him the speed limit was twenty-five, and then he asked me how to get to the Rocking Diamond."

"A big white one, with a comealong on the front?" Julie asked.

"*Ja,*" he said in surprise. "How did you know?"

"I was at the bishop's today helping Sadie and Ruby make blackberry jam," Julie said. "The Yoder boys were underfoot until the bishop chased them off. Anyway, I saw Trey Madison pulling a pickup like that out of the ditch with his big red truck."

"Guess he should have listened," he said.

"I heard Trey call him Cord. Do you know who that is?"

Alden shook his head. "He can't be very experienced if he plans to hire on at the Rocking Diamond. He sits his hat on its brim."

Julie waved this away. "No, silly. Don't you read the papers? That had to be Cord McLean, that movie star who's here to learn how to be a cowboy for his next film."

"Did one of those girls at the Safeway tell you that?" Beth asked in surprise.

Julie was friends with a couple of the checkout clerks who played hockey at the community center in the winter. Julie would never join the team because of the uniform requirements, but she sometimes went to cheer them on.

"Neh," Julie said. "I read it in *The Western News.*" She pointed at the stack of papers in their box next to the woodstove, which they used as fire starter and which Alden never had time to read.

Maybe he ought to make time.

"Even movie stars have to obey the speed limit," Mamm said, apparently not caring much about Cord McLean or his truck. *"Denki* for lunch. I need to get back. I'm expecting UPS with some new fabric and I don't want them to just leave it at the door."

After Mamm had gone, and while the girls washed the lunch dishes, Alden fished yesterday's paper out of the box. There it was, right on the front page, with a picture of the young man who had nearly clipped him on Main Street. Definitely the kind of face that girls remembered.

Cord McLean to Arrive This Week

Libby, MT — Fans in Lincoln County will be keeping an eye on the highways this week, watching for Cord McLean's arrival in the Siksika Valley. *The Western News* has discovered that he's scheduled to spend a month at the Rocking Diamond Ranch with a professional trainer, learning aspects of horsemanship, ranch management, and cattle wrangling in preparation for shooting his next film.

As readers of this paper will remember, he is set to star in an adaptation of the 1942 novel *Ride Forever* by mystery novelist Lee Bateson. His co-stars include Millie Bobby Brown and Harrison Ford, but it is not expected that they will be joining him for what he has nicknamed "cowboy training."

Mrs Taylor Madison, co-owner of the ranch, graciously confirmed that the star was expected this week. "He'll be treated just like any other guest on the Rocking Diamond," she said, "and will be staying in one of our comfortable guest rooms in the main house. Should he prefer to maintain his privacy in one of our cabins, one has been set aside for him, but it could be that his staff will be housed there. We'll have to wait and see. In any case, we're eager to welcome him and introduce him to the grandeur of Montana, and in particular the stunning beauty of the Rocking Diamond Ranch."

When asked if Mr McLean would be granting interviews during his visit, Mrs Madison was unable to confirm. "I'll pass on your request, of course," she said with a smile. "But there's a lot to learn in order to play a real cowboy convincingly. We're going to keep him pretty busy."

Ride Forever will be released in theaters next year.

His staff? The guy had been alone in his truck. But that didn't mean anything—if he had a staff, they could be coming separately. Didn't matter. The important thing was, now that it was known a movie star was in the valley, they'd likely get more tourist traffic, which could only benefit the businesses along Main Street. Maybe even swell the crowd at the school auction on Saturday.

As he walked to his shop and got back to work on the Rocking Diamond's front gates, Alden didn't know whether to be happy about more people seeing Malena's quilt, or sad that it would likely go out of state to an *Englisch* person's home.

Which reminded him ...

While the wrought iron cooled enough to be handled, he went to the table near the front door that did duty as his office, rifled through the invoices and orders on it to locate his cell phone, and tapped in the number he had memorized. The ranchers had cell phones for times like roundup or riding fence miles from the house. Bishop Joe was a practical man, and had no desire for any of his flock to freeze to death while trying to save a calf because they couldn't call for help. Alden needed this phone for his business, since half the time he was out in the farrier's wagon.

"Circle M," Reuben Miller grunted into the phone that hung in the barn.

"*Guder mariye*, Reuben," he said easily. "Alden Stolzfus here. I'm calling about shoeing your two cutting horses before roundup. I had a job fall out, so is tomorrow *gut* for you?"

"*Ja.*" Reuben was a man of few words. "Eight o'clock?"

"I'll be there."

"You'll have time for coffee after? The girls will whip up something special if they know you're coming."

Alden doubted he had that effect on any woman, but it was nice of Reuben to say so. "Anything they make tastes *gut*. See you then."

"Say, Alden?"

"*Ja?*"

"Have you heard anything about some movie star coming to the Rocking Diamond?"

The Amish grapevine was as good as the *Englisch* TV. "Just what was in *The Western News* yesterday. Oh, and I met the guy this morning. Nearly shaved some weight off me, speeding on Main Street. Seemed civil enough."

"Huh."

There had to be more to this. "Why?"

"He bummed a ride from Malena this morning. Ran his truck into the ditch and she gave him a lift up to Madisons'."

Alden's hand tightened around the phone. "Is she all right?"

"Oh, sure. She laughed about it. But I'll be happy if the Madisons keep him to themselves. See you tomorrow."

He hung up, and Alden clicked off his own phone before he ambled back to his ironwork. He tried to picture Cord McLean hitching a ride in an Amish buggy, but his imagination failed him. He'd sure like to know what Malena thought of him —if anything.

It was just like her to offer a stranded person a ride, even someone who had put his flashy truck in the ditch out of sheer stupidity.

From what the paper said, it wasn't likely anyone would see much of their famous guest. If he knew the Madisons, they'd keep him all to themselves.

Well, they were welcome to him. Everybody else had real work to do.

THE NEXT MORNING, THE STOLZFUS HOUSEHOLD WAS UP well before dawn. Mamm always made sure Alden had a hot breakfast before they went to work, but on his days away, she also packed a lunch into a plastic tub in case the job ran long. If he was working on an Amish place, when mealtime rolled around he'd be invited in for lunch. But if his customers were

Englisch, it could go either way. Some days that little tub of food was mighty welcome.

He figured he'd be back home by lunchtime today, though, what with all the work left to do on the gates. Technically, he should have finished them before he took a day away to do farrier work, but something inside had urged him out to the Circle M.

He'd learned not to ignore that still, small voice, even when its promptings didn't make sense at the time. They always did afterward.

So, eight o'clock found him behind Joseph, the big Belgian draft horse he'd bought to pull the heavy farrier's wagon, rolling up the lane of the Circle M. Reuben Miller came out of the barn doors as he approached, and motioned for him to back the wagon up to the corral gate, where Delphinium and Marigold were already waiting. The Miller twins had named the cutting horses after flowers when they were younger, when their parents had made the mistake of assigning that coveted duty to them. Adam and Zach had been considerate enough of the gelding's dignity to call him Del. Marigold, fortunately, was a mare and her name suited her. These were smart, active animals who were important contributors to the success of the ranch.

And trimmed hooves and comfortable shoes helped them do their jobs.

The rear of the wagon filled the open gateway in the corral fence, so his tools were in easy reach and the horses couldn't slip past. Today's job was fairly light; just hoof trims and shoe replacements for two horses who were easy to work with. He got the generator going, and while the traveling forge heated up, put on his leather chaps and chose today's picks and clippers from their drawers. Del and Marigold were polite horses who were used to him, so cleaning and trimming didn't take long.

On some places, like the Rocking Diamond, he could be there all day tending to the strings of horses used for trail rides. Doc MacDonald, the large-animal vet who served a wide area around the Siksika, had an office in Mountain Home, and was also a farrier. When it came to the Rocking Diamond, they usually partnered up simply because there was so much work that one man couldn't finish in a day, or even two. The Madisons believed in good foot hygiene for their herd. Even so, the vet often found small injuries that needed to be treated before the horse could go back to work, and Alden was glad to learn. He was no vet, but if he could take care of an injury, that would save MacDonald a trip.

Alden was finishing up the last of Marigold's shoes when the sound of horses approaching made the mare toss her head. He tightened his knees to signal to her that her hoof was still under his care, and she snorted.

There had been no sound of buggy wheels, he realized. That meant the riders were not Amish, who only rode for work, not to visit or for recreation. And what would bring *Englisch* riders to the Circle M?

But these questions couldn't be answered while he had a horse's forefoot trapped between his knees. He finished with the shoe and released Marigold. "Good girl," he said, smiling.

She huffed out a breath and cantered away to the opposite gate, which led back to the pasture. Reuben let her and Del out into the home field, where they kicked up their heels as though to try out their new shoes. Still smiling at the sight, Alden turned and found the riders waiting at the bars of the corral, watching him.

Trey Madison and Cord McLean.

Well, of all things, as his *Grossmammi* used to say.

"Can I help you boys?" Reuben called, closing the far gate with a clang. He ambled up.

Since this was Reuben's ranch and his visitors were none of Alden's business, he took care to mind his own. It took time to clean and put away the tools and the old shoes, make sure there were no nails left on the ground, and shut down the forge.

"Morning," Trey finally said. "I see Stolzfus is here to shoe your horses."

"Yep," Reuben said, as though it wasn't completely obvious. "Something I can do for you?"

"Reuben Miller, Alden Stolzfus, this is Cord McLean. He's here for horse and cattle training. Prepping for his new movie."

Reuben reached up and shook his hand. Alden merely nodded. But he couldn't resist saying, "I heard you had some trouble with your truck yesterday."

When he shut off the generator, the sounds of birdsong and Joseph's teeth tugging at the grass flowed into the silence, along with the creak of saddle leather and the clearing of Trey's throat.

"Well, that's one of the reasons we're here," Trey said. "Cord wanted to thank Malena for giving him a lift to our place."

"I expect he already did thank her." Reuben gazed up at them as though wondering why they were burning daylight.

"Thank her *again*," Cord said, emphasizing the final word. "It was kind of her to give a stranger a ride."

"This isn't the city," Alden pointed out. "Folks will stop to help if they can. Like Trey helping you pull the truck out of the ditch."

ADINA SENFT

"You're well informed," Cord said, a pleat forming between his brows, as though he didn't know people were already talking over his arrival.

"My sister was on her way home and saw you," Alden said. "This is a small place. Everything is news. People speeding on sharp curves, for instance."

"I consider myself warned," Cord said. "Again. So, is she around this morning?"

But instead of answering, Reuben said, "That's one reason. You said there was another?"

Trey and the actor glanced at one another. Finally Trey tipped his head as if to say, *All right. All yours.*

"Well, something has come up—or maybe I should say, it hasn't come up," Cord began. His horse shifted under him, and again the saddle leather creaked. "We expected my trainer to be here when I arrived yesterday, but he wasn't. We heard this morning that he was in a car accident on the way here, outside of Great Falls."

"Is he okay?" Alden asked.

"Banged up, possibly a concussion and a broken wrist," Cord said. "The bottom line is, he won't be coming for at least a week, maybe more. I only have three weeks to train before we start shooting, so losing a week is going to affect my ability to do the part as well as I want to."

Reuben gazed at him, puzzled. "Grayson's a pretty good trainer. Teaches hundreds of greenhorns to ride, some of them well. Won't he do?"

"He's full up with the guests on the ranch," Trey said. "Plus there's a corporate retreat starting Saturday, and he's leading them up onto the allotment for a three-day ride."

"All right. So you're short-handed. Is that why you're here? Because so am I."

THE AMISH COWBOY'S MAKEOVER

Adam Miller had gone back to Pennsylvania to help the family of his special friend Kate Weaver with harvest ... and to court her properly. Alden couldn't imagine that Zach, Joshua, and Daniel would have enough time at this, their busiest season of the year, to teach a movie star how to be a cowboy. The very idea was laughable.

"Well, that's part of it," Cord said earnestly. He leaned forward a little in the saddle, and his horse took an uncertain step, his chest up against the corral rails.

Alden put out a hand to stop the animal. "He thinks you want him to walk on. Sit back."

When he did, the horse backed away obediently, a little relieved that this time the command made sense.

"Now, see? That's just the kind of thing I need to know," Cord said. "So if my trainer is in the hospital, and the Rocking Diamond trainer is committed to other guests, and you folks are short-handed, what are our other options?"

If Reuben's face was any indication, there was no *our* here. This was not the Circle M's problem. If anything, it was the movie people's problem, wherever or whoever they were.

"Seems you'd best free up Grayson, and send one of the hands up the mountain with these corporate people," Reuben said at last, since no one else spoke.

Trey shook his head. "No can do. The CEO is a friend of Dad's, and he promised him the best the ranch could offer. And our best isn't one of the summer hands. Or me or my brothers."

"Looks like you're in a pickle, son," Reuben said to Cord.

"Not necessarily," the young man said. "Not if I could come here instead. If someone could teach me how to ride and rope, I could work with your sons. I could learn from them just about everything I need to know."

An incredulous silence blew along the wind.

But Cord wasn't finished. "The best part is, an Amish ranch is probably the closest I'll ever come to the way life was lived in 1942. I could probably even learn how to shoe a horse from my good buddy Alden here."

Alden nearly dropped the heavy pliers on his own foot.

$\maltese$ 4 $\maltese$

MALENA'S JAW hung open like a broken gate as Cord McLean, Trey Madison, and Alden Stolzfus all trooped into the kitchen behind her father. Alden they'd expected—and there was a cinnamon-apple cake with maple sugar frosting to prove it. Malena had seen how much he'd enjoyed the one she'd brought to a singing earlier in the year, and since the Transparent up in Grossmammi's orchard was ready to pick, the decision had been easy.

After the introductions, she and Rebecca exchanged an amazed glance, and then got busy putting more plates and coffee mugs on the big kitchen table as their guests sat down. Zach and Joshua came in, and Sara brought in baby Nathan on one hip and their almost five-month-old sister Deborah on the other, and suddenly the table was full again, the way it hadn't been since Daniel had got married and Adam had gone east with Kate.

The yellow checkered tablecloth and the bouquet of wild-flowers Rebecca had picked this morning looked well with Mamm's blue and white coffee set. Hmm. Yellow and blue and white was such a summery, happy combination. Just a tiny bit of spring green would set it off. Could she do something with her Montana Star pattern and—

"Smells great in here," Cord said with a grin across the table at Malena. "Did you have something to do with that?"

She came out of her thoughts with a bump. "*Ja,*" she said, and blurted, "Alden likes this apple cake."

Alden sat up straighter in surprise. Maybe it was a new experience for someone to notice what he liked. And maybe it was a new experience for Cord when someone noticed someone who wasn't *him*.

Alden was such a loner, always busy in his shop, that he didn't run around much with the *Youngie*. He had a reputation among the *Maedscher* for kindness and a good sense of humor, and Malena knew more than one who would have said yes to a ride home with him after singing. But he didn't seem to have time for a special friend.

Mamm cut the cake in generous pieces and handed the plates around, then a plate of delicious round cheeses made by the bachelor Zook brothers. A basket of her famous cheese-and-green-chile muffins, fresh out of the oven and hot enough to melt butter, followed.

"This is amazing, Mrs Miller," Trey said with his mouth full. "Thanks."

"It's just a little *kaffee*," Mamm said, though she looked pleased as she handed him the butter. "My family has a full day. They can't work on an empty stomach. Neither can Alden, after coming out from town to look after our horses."

"Seems Cord and Trey want to make us a proposal, Naomi," Dat said. "I didn't want to give them an answer until you'd heard it, too."

If this proposal had been about ranch work, Dat would

simply have made a decision and sent them on their way. It must be about something else. Something bigger. Or more complicated, if it involved everyone in the family. Malena listened with interest as Cord began to speak. Interest changed to surprise, and then downright disbelief. When he got to the part about Alden teaching him to shoe a horse, she caught Alden's eye.

Something about the barely concealed horror she saw there gave her the giggles. She tried to stifle them. Even stuffed a big bite of muffin in her mouth to stop them.

It wasn't polite to laugh at a man's crack-brained ideas. *Ach, neh*, this was as bad as getting the giggles in church. She mustn't laugh—he was a guest, and she mustn't hurt his feelings. But then the corners of Alden's lips twitched.

She swallowed the muffin with a big gulp of coffee. Barely got it down before she made a sound like a horse's whinny, and completely lost it. Clapping a napkin to her face, she laughed, and the expression now on Alden's face—humor mixed with despair at the fate this young man was so blithely proposing for him—only made her laugh harder.

And then Rebecca joined in, and Zach guffawed, and in two seconds the only two people not in fits of laughter were Cord McLean and Trey Madison.

Poor Cord. People probably didn't laugh much when he was around. He gazed at them all, clearly wondering where the joke was, and smiling in a lame sort of way.

"I'm sorry, Cord," she gasped. "I don't mean to laugh, but—"

Even the babies had caught the giggles! A whoop came out of Malena's throat and a big fat tear trickled down her flushed face. She had to get hold of herself. She'd started it—she and Alden.

She glared at him. "Stop it," she begged. "Cord is serious."

That was the funny part—the poor *Englisch mann* didn't see how ridiculous it was that he could even ask. She almost felt sorry for him. He'd come to the only place in the country, probably, where hardly anyone knew who he was, and even if they did, they had no time to cater to him and his silly film.

The person she did feel sorry for was his trainer, in hospital in Great Falls. Now, that was something serious.

Her family found some self-control from somewhere, and Malena took a few deep breaths. If she could avoid catching Alden's eye again, she might have a chance at acting her age.

"We apologize, Cord," Mamm finally said, recovering enough to cut him another piece of apple cake. "But what you're proposing is so completely impossible it just struck us as funny. Please don't take it personally. We don't mean it that way."

"I'm trying not to," he said. "But maybe you can help me understand why it's so impossible? I learn fast—I've only ridden a horse a couple of times before, and I made it over here all right."

"It's a matter of the hours in the day," Dat said. The humor faded from his eyes and the atmosphere at the table became more businesslike. "If someone takes an hour to show you how to rope, that's an hour of fence repair that doesn't get done. If someone takes you with them to teach you how to string wire, that's two hours of working the sluices left undone. All of a sudden we've lost three hours of work. Multiply that by the thirty or so days we have until roundup, and what do you get?"

Cord did the arithmetic. "Ninety hours of training?"

"Two weeks of work left undone," Zach corrected him.

"Hey, that's not fair," Cord protested. "You're thinking that those hours are just teaching me. But what if they're not?

What if they're me helping? Lending an extra pair of hands? Once I learn something, I can work as hard as any of you, and make up those hours."

"Define *hard*," Sara said unexpectedly. "I'm one of the few Amish in the valley who has lived in the *Englisch* world. I was an EMT—still am. I know about working nights and twelve-hour shifts, which you're probably familiar with too, in your business. But that's different from ranch work, where you're using your hands and your brains from before sunup to after sunset. Without electricity, trucks, or power tools. It's a whole other world out here, Cord."

It had been a long time since Sara had made such a long speech.

"But it's a world I need to know to play this part," he said.

"Ranch life ain't play," Reuben said. "I suspect that's where you're making your mistake. Something like leaving a gate open or opening the wrong sluice can mean an animal dies. Using a tool without protective gear can mean losing a finger— or a hand. Not communicating properly with your horse can mean injury to a valuable animal. Everything we do carries a risk."

"But you learn how to do those things," he argued. "Maybe you start as kids—I know I don't have that advantage. I'm a midwestern city kid. But I'm strong and I think I'm smart. My agent says I'm too smart for my own good."

Nobody had a reply to this. Malena had lost the urge to laugh.

"Please," Cord said. "Just a week. Give me a week's trial. If you find that you lose more hours than I help you make up, cut me loose. By then Grayson will be back, or my trainer will be well enough to come. I promise you that I won't waste your time."

Dat gazed at him. Then turned his gaze to Mamm. In that strange way of communication they had, they made a decision.

She got up and fetched the coffee pot, and refilled Cord's cup.

"Thank you, ma'am," he said, his voice subdued, as though he'd run out of steam and had no points left to press.

"We're Amish," she told him gently. "We don't use honorifics. You can call me Naomi."

"Naomi," he repeated.

"You can stay for a week," Dat said. Malena could see what this cost him—what it would cost all of them—balancing the lost hours against their powerful neighbor's goodwill.

Trey sat back, beaming. "Great. He can ride over every day and—"

"Nope." With another glance at Mamm, he said to Cord, "If you want to live like it's 1942, you'll stay here, in the spare room. Up at four for chores. Breakfast at five. Zach and Malena will be in charge of you."

Zach smiled as though it hurt him. Malena nearly blurted, "Why me?" but bit the words back just in time. If Dat said she was to babysit this young man, then babysit she would. Rebecca almost smiled, too—until the moment she realized that all Malena's work in house and garden was about to land on her own slender shoulders.

Cord swallowed. "What about time off? Weekends?"

"There's only one weekend in the next seven days," Dat pointed out. "The school auction is Saturday, and we all plan to go after chores. You can go or not, as you like, as long as you're back for evening chores. Sunday we don't have church, but it's a family day with visiting church members, so you can go to the Rocking Diamond and have a day off. We'll look after the chores. Monday, it's back to work."

"Can you handle that?" Trey asked him, looking a little dubious.

"Yep," Cord said.

Malena would believe it when she saw it.

"Now that's settled," Dat said, draining his coffee cup and pushing back from the table, "maybe one of the girls has some time this morning to give you a riding lesson. Then you can go down to our son Daniel's place and ask his boy Joel to show you how to rope a calf."

DAT HAD TAUGHT ALL OF THEM HOW TO RIDE A CUTTING horse when their legs were long enough to put their feet in the stirrups and control the animal. But even before that, one of Malena's earliest memories was whistling up a horse and rewarding him with a cut-up apple, then being lifted onto its back so she could see the ranch the way he did.

She figured that was the way to begin with the greenhorn.

"I know how to ride," he protested, as he followed her into the pasture, where Delphinium and Marigold eyed them in surprise at this break from routine.

She lifted a hand to wave at Alden as the farrier's departing buggy came into sight on the road, headed back to his shop in Mountain Home. She could just see him wave out the window before the stand of pines concealed him again.

They could hear the clop of Trey's horse heading off down the lane, too, leading the one Cord had ridden over. He'd be back with Cord's bags. By then, Malena hoped to have made some progress.

She turned her attention once more to her student. "You may know how to ride, but these horses aren't waiting in a nice air-conditioned stall for you to tack up. Here, you call the horse over, take him to the barn, and saddle him there. Or her, in this case. You'll be working with Marigold, the mare."

"Which one is the mare?"

"The lighter, reddish one. The dun is Del—he's a gelding. That means—"

"I know what it means."

"*Gut.* Go and get her. Introduce yourself so she knows your voice. Take this." She held out some apple pieces from the baking earlier.

"Nah, I don't need those. She'll come to me. I have a way with horses. Did you ever see *Race the Bluegrass?*"

"We don't go to movies."

"It's a western adventure I did about a carriage race in Kentucky."

That must be why he was so familiar with getting in and out of a buggy. But had his training then included calling and hitching up a horse?

Ten minutes later, she had her answer. The apple pieces were nearly gone and Marigold was having a wonderful time with this new game. Cord was red-faced and sweating. "Don't give her the apple until she listens, Cord. I promise it works. She loves them."

He did as she said without much grace, and sure enough, Marigold came trotting up to nuzzle his hand and claim her reward as though her bad behavior had been some other horse's. He had the foresight to grab her halter before she finished crunching it, and they were able to lead her into the barn.

Tacking up the horse was more about common sense than anything—blanket, for instance, then saddle—but even so, he wrote down everything she said in a tiny notebook from his pocket, complete with diagrams. Until she took all the tack off and put it back in its place.

"Your turn."

Another half hour went by before Marigold was once again fit for work and Cord was mounted up. "Now what? Roping calves?"

"That would be putting the calf before the horse. We could do lead training here in the corral, or you could do it on the road over to Daniel's."

"The road," he said. "Two things at once. Saves your time."

"I'll get the gates. Remember what Alden said. If you lean forward, she'll think you want her to pick up her pace. Lean back, and she'll come to a stop. We'll learn some more cues in a minute."

Marigold knew the way to Daniel's and to Joel, who was one of her favorite people. Cord had to practice leaning back to slow her down.

"Time to show this horse who's boss," he said, frowning.

"You don't need to do that." Since she wasn't dressed for riding, with jeans and boots under her dress, Malena walked beside him. She gave Marigold a reassuring pat on the neck. "You and she are partners. Once she knows what you intend to do, she'll do it. It's your job to communicate with her, not treat her like furniture."

"So how do I do that, horse whisperer?"

She'd heard that expression before from Josh. She still wasn't sure what it meant, except for someone who communicated with horses. Which her father and brothers did all day long.

"With your legs." She showed him the three basic leg positions and Marigold obediently demonstrated what they meant. Malena made him repeat them, over and over, until she could see from the horse's growing comfort that muscle memory was being formed in the stranger on her back.

"I'm going to feel this tomorrow," he groaned.

"*Ja*, you sure are." He gave her a dirty look for agreeing with him. "Next thing. The horse has two sides. The near side and the off side. To get her to turn toward a cow, open your hand in the cow's direction and push her with the near-side knee. I'll be the cow."

"You're way too pretty to be a cow."

"Marigold doesn't care," she said, ignoring him. "She just wants me cut out of my herd. Ready?"

Marigold beat him to it. Malena zigzagged across the road, the horse anticipating her. Cord lost his seat and had slithered halfway out of the saddle before he grabbed the horn and dragged himself upright.

"Whoa, Marigold," Malena said soothingly as the horse came to a stop. "We have to slow down. He's just a beginner." To Cord, she said, "Let's do some circles and turns."

The circles and turns took them most of the way to Daniel and Lovina's house. But at least when she tried the zigzag again, he was familiar enough with Marigold to let her do her job and simply hang on.

He bit back an "Umph!" of muscle soreness as he dismounted and tied Marigold to the new fence that protected Lovina's garden from everything from chickens to cattle.

"You did well," Malena told him. "Most people think riding is done with the arms and back. But with working ranch horses, it's all in the core of your stomach, legs, and hips. You'll get used to it. By the end of the week, you won't be feeling it as much."

"Thanks," he muttered, and limped after her.

Lovina came out on the newly finished back porch, which

replaced the cement block they'd been using as a step. "Hallo, Malena," she said, wiping her hands on a dish towel. "Is this the young man I've heard about?"

"*Ja*. Cord McLean, this is my brother's wife, Lovina Miller."

Cord tugged his hat brim with two fingers. "Nice to meet you, ma—Lovina."

"Cord is doing some cowboy training for a film," Malena said, "and will be staying at the house for a week. I'm teaching him how to ride so he can go out with Zach and Daniel."

"He doesn't know how to ride?"

"He's doing pretty well for a greenhorn," Malena allowed. "Dat thought Joel might enjoy teaching him how to rope a cow."

A smile flooded Lovina's face. "He sure would. He practices every day on the one in the barn if there isn't a live one handy. Come inside, both of you. I just took peanut butter chocolate chip cookies out of the oven."

"Great," Cord said, following his hostess into the kitchen like a bird dog on a scent. "Is Joel around now?"

Lovina shook her head and looked behind her, as though she might be overheard. Her eyes twinkled. "I think the two of them and Zach snuck down to the river for a quick swim before lunch. I heard them hollering a little while ago."

It was a warm day, all right, and even though the boys were probably hollering at the cold water, it would still be welcome. She couldn't blame them for taking a break. To Cord, she said, "My brothers have been working the sluices since breakfast, with Joel along as helper."

"Does that have something to do with water?" When Lovina offered them a plate of warm cookies, he took two.

Malena snagged one for herself. "The irrigation system in

the pastures. Once one field is watered, you direct the sluices to the next. All summer long. Every day."

"We're lucky here, to have the river so close," Lovina put in, helping herself to a cookie. "Out east of Great Falls, some of the ranches don't, and have to depend on rain."

"Will I be working the sluices?"

"You heard me say *every day*? You'll probably be out there at some time or another." Malena took another cookie. They were so rich and buttery, they melted in the mouth. She turned to her *Schwei*. "Maybe Cord can come down after lunch for some roping practice? He doesn't have to stay all afternoon if you need Joel."

Lovina nodded. "I'll tell him," she said.

"These are really good," Cord mumbled, his mouth full, as he reached for another cookie.

"Thank you." She smiled at him. "You could use some fattening up. Help yourself."

He froze, and withdrew his hand. "I guess not. Thanks, though. The camera puts twenty-five pounds on a person. My dresser will have my head if they have to let out all my wardrobe."

Malena was trying to imagine how a camera could make a person put on weight, when the timer on the counter pinged and Lovina got up to take another sheet of cookies out of the propane oven.

Poor Cord. He looked like the chickens did when she came in with the vegetable trimmings for the pigs. Hopeful, even when they knew the goodies weren't for them. She took pity on him and got up. "Thanks, Lovina. Time for some more turns and circles."

He followed her outside, untied Marigold, and mounted up. "She's a nice lady," he offered, using an open hand and a field-side knee to turn Marigold and point her up the road. "I'm going to have to watch my weight around here, I can tell already. How come the whole family isn't overweight if they eat, like, five times a day?"

"We work," she told him flatly. "A lot. All day long."

"What do you do for fun?"

"Play volleyball. Swim. Hike. Once the work is done."

"I get it." He lengthened his next circle as they moved into the cool shadows of the pines. "But what about other stuff for fun?"

"Like what?" She did a zigzag across the road, but he was ready for her, keeping his seat while Marigold went to work.

"Not movies, I guess. Or going to a bar. I don't know—going to town for ice cream?"

She zagged the other way, and Marigold stopped her.

"Good girl." She patted the horse's shoulder and walked beside her. "We make ice cream here, depending on what's in the garden. You haven't lived until you've tasted my sister's raspberry lemonade ice cream."

He took the Lord's name in vain in a longing kind of voice, and she tapped him on the knee. "Please don't do that. God's name is sacred."

"Sorry."

He actually looked it, but then, he was an actor.

"We'll be going to singing on Sunday."

"What's that?"

"It's at Bontragers' this week. The next place, there." They emerged from the trees, and she pointed across the river, past the fields beyond it. The Bontrager home was a mile away, concealed behind a grassy hill. "We sing for a couple of hours, then have supper. Mind you, it's in *Deitsch* mostly, but we sing a few *Englisch* songs. Like 'Take Me Home,

Country Roads.' And 'How Great Thou Art.' I like the old *Englisch* hymns."

"You sing hymns for fun?"

She wasn't sure if he was making fun of her, or asking because he really wanted to know.

Give him a little grace, Malena, Mamm would have said. *He doesn't know our ways, just like you don't know his.*

That was for sure and certain. She went with the second option. "*Ja.* It's *gut* to praise God together. And it's fun to just be us, just the *Youngie*—that means young folks." She eyed him. "Maybe that's too tame for you. But we like it."

"What are the odds that people sang glees in their parlors in 1942? Practically every movie Judy Garland made in the forties was a musical, right?"

"I don't know," she said steadily. What was a glee? And who was Judy Garland? Never mind. "Sunday is your day off. Probably the Madison boys will take you to Whitefish and show you a good time."

"Yeah," he said vaguely, as though this was the first it had occurred to him. "But that's not going to give me the experience I want, is it? I can go to Mammoth or Breckenridge. These weeks are for training."

"Look, there are Daniel and Joel." She pointed to the swimming hole at the big bend in the river meadows, where her brother and nephew were coming along the trail. Both were barefoot, carrying their boots. "That was a pretty fast swim."

"Is the water cold?"

She laughed. "It's glacier melt. But it feels *gut* when you're sweaty and tired."

"So there is time for fun. Without hymns. Maybe I can go swimming, too, when I've learned my lessons for today."

"Maybe."

He glanced at her. "Do you think I can do this?"

How would she know what he was capable of? If he couldn't, it wouldn't be the fault of anyone on the Circle M. "By the end of the week you might fool anybody into thinking you're a cowboy," she assured him, only half believing it.

✨ 5 ✨

HER YOUNGEST HALF asleep in her arms, Naomi stood in the doorway of the guest room across the hall from hers and Reuben's, looking it over to satisfy herself it was ready for their unexpected guest. Cord's bags sat on the floor—six of them. Since the closet was not very large, she hoped the dresser would be sufficient to hold whatever was in there. Imagine six bags for only three weeks. One Amish person would never be able to manage all that on a train.

But he'd likely come to Montana on an airplane. Maybe things were different in airports. She'd never been in one, since the Amish didn't fly, though she harbored a secret desire to fly in a plane, just once, so she might see the world as God saw it.

One thing was for sure—it would keep a person humble.

She bent to smooth a ripple from the quilt, which was one of Malena's. She had designed a Mariner's Compass for Elizabeth Weaver, thinking the girl was going to marry Adam, but that hadn't happened. Nor had Elizabeth really loved the design. But Malena had loved it enough to make it up anyway, and here it was to welcome their guests, the pattern a melding

48

of star and flower that took Naomi's breath away every time she passed the door.

The racket in the kitchen increased as the men came in from washing up, which meant Naomi had to stop daydreaming and put little Deborah down for her nap. With a kiss and a deep breath of her sweet baby smell, Naomi left her in her crib and closed her bedroom door quietly.

When the big pot of elk stew was on the table, along with hot biscuits, mashed potatoes, a big salad, fresh-baked bread, and the last of the carrot pickles from last year, she seated herself at Reuben's right hand. Their guest looked as though he didn't know what to do when the family bowed their heads in a silent grace, but at least he had enough respect to sit quietly until Reuben raised his head.

Naomi loved to see her family enjoying their food. Elk stew was a surprise, because she usually made it for large neighborhood occasions like roundup in the autumn or turnout in the spring, or when they had church here. The chatter rose, knives and forks clattered, and spoons clacked in bowls as Sara dished up for everyone. Joshua held little Nathan, who was growing like a dandelion. He'd be a year old before they knew it, and was looking like he wanted to walk already.

She noticed that while Cord McLean took a good portion of stew, he passed on the biscuits and heaped his plate with salad instead. While he had muscles, it was clear, he was more lean than muscular, and carried no extra fat. Ach, well, he'd learn quickly enough that food was fuel, and dieting was for the paying guests over at the Rocking Diamond.

"So, Cord, how did the roping lessons go?" Zach asked when he'd polished off his first helping of stew and was holding out his plate for another.

Cord leveled an accusing glance at Malena. "*Somebody*

neglected to tell me I'd be roping a hay bale," he said. "I thought I was going to rope a calf."

"We don't have a calf to spare," Zach said mildly.

"There's a whole ranch full of them," Cord objected.

"They're up on the allotment, grazing and getting fat, not running and being stressed about a stranger chasing them," Joshua said.

"They don't stay still as well as hay bales," Rebecca agreed.

Cord took a deep breath and visibly controlled the urge to argue. "Anyway, the lessons went well. Joel is a good teacher. It only took me an hour of trying before I got the rope over the horns."

"You wouldn't have managed that with a calf," Reuben pointed out, buttering another slice of bread. Naomi pushed a jar of the blackberry jam the girls had been making at the bishop's closer to him.

"No," Cord was forced to agree. "But I hope it won't be long before I do."

"Once you can drop the lasso over those horns four or five times in a row," Zach said, "we can think about putting you on a horse."

"In the pasture?" Their guest gave in to the blandishment of the biscuits, and took one as though it might still be hot. A man had to mop up his gravy with something besides mashed potatoes.

"No, in the corral," Malena said. "You'll rope a bale from horseback."

"Another bale?" he exclaimed. "This is going to take forever."

"That depends on you," Reuben said. "Roping a still object from horseback ain't as difficult as roping a moving one, but it still ain't easy. You'll be managing a horse as well as a rope, each of them going in different directions."

"It'll take you couple of days, I expect," Zach said. "In your spare time. After the sluices in the morning, we need to go up on the allotment and make sure the collection pens are ready for roundup. Repair any fences that need it. You up for that?"

"Yes," Cord said.

Naomi suspected he would have said so whether he was ready or not.

"Ever handled pliers and wire?"

"No."

Zach nodded. "You can use Adam's gloves. Otherwise your hands will get torn up and roping will be harder."

"Good to know."

Since his replies were getting shorter the more he realized what he'd signed on for, Naomi took pity on him and turned the conversation to other things. When the girls cleared the table, he offered to dry dishes for Malena, but Sara and Rebecca cut him out of the group as neatly as Marigold ever separated a calf from its herd, and he wound up in the living room with the men. The dishes would go much faster without him.

He declined to stay for Bible reading, and instead made his way down the short hall to the guest room. Every step hurt, Naomi could see that.

Half an hour later, when Reuben closed the old Bible and they rose to get ready for bed or do some quiet work by lamplight, Naomi took Sara aside. "You'd better look out some liniment for our greenhorn," she said in a low tone. "He seems pretty sore."

"I was thinking that, too. When he gets out of the shower, I'll give him some, and show him how to apply it."

Out of the corner of her eye, Naomi saw Malena go out the kitchen door. Not in her usual always-in-a-hurry way, but slowly, thoughtfully. There was a time to leave a young woman alone, and a time to be a companion. Naomi thought that this might be the latter.

She followed her daughter outside, closing the door and breathing in the scents of a summer night in the high country. Pine sap, grass, dust, and gently laid over it, the flowers she grew in pots close to the house, where the wind wouldn't tear at them and the animals wouldn't eat them.

Malena was leaning on the rail, gazing out over the rocks and meadows toward the little plateau where Adam planned to build his and Kate's home next year.

"Want some company?" she asked gently, leaning on the rail next to her.

"I wouldn't chase you away." Malena smiled, and breathed deeply. "I love that smell. Pine pitch after the heat of the day."

"Me too. And my spoiled-rotten stock and sweet alyssum smell so good. It's like they're giving all they can because they know their lives are short."

"Worth spoiling them for, then," Malena agreed. "That only works with flowers. Not so much with people."

"Are you talking about a certain person who might be a little saddle sore this evening?"

"I might be. What happened there, when we did the dishes?"

"I think your *Schweschdere* don't want him to get too comfortable. He might be a tiny bit sweet on you."

Malena snorted, sounding exactly like Bachelor Button when he saw a snake. "Impossible."

"I wouldn't say that," Naomi reflected, directing her

remarks to the view. "I think you're pretty easy to love, but then, I'm biased."

"I'm not going to fall in love with an *Englischer*, Mamm."

"I know, *Liewi*. But there are some men that fall in love for a hobby. If he's that kind, it would be wise not to encourage anything more than a..." She searched for the right word. "Businesslike friendship."

"Believe me, teaching him how to ride is more business than friendship ... or anything else."

"I believe it," Naomi said with a chuckle. "Poor man."

"Speaking of friends, it was *gut* that Alden was able to stop for *Kaffee* this morning. He doesn't socialize much. I wonder if Cord was serious about learning to shoe a horse."

"Cord is going to have enough on his plate learning to ride his horse, never mind figuring out what goes on its feet."

"But if he was, we might see a bit more of Alden."

Naomi kept her voice light. "He works hard, that young man. Being a smith and a farrier is work as hard as ranching."

"Except you don't have to do it in a howling blizzard ... most of the time."

"I'm glad Rose Stolzfus brought her family to the Siksika," Naomi said. "She gave you *gut* advice about your quilts. When are you taking the Glacier Lily over to the school?"

"I told my helpers the quilts needed to be in the tent by seven. The gates open at eight, and the quilt auction starts at eleven. We want to give people time to look them over."

"It will be exciting. Are all the *Youngie* planning to go?"

"All that can," Malena said. "Rose told me she's closing up shop because the likelihood of someone buying a quilt there when so many beautiful ones are up for auction is pretty low. Yoder's Variety Store isn't closing, but the girls have the day off. Same with the Bitterroot Dutch Café—Susan is going while her mother stays."

"I hope Alden closes up the smithy, too," Naomi said innocently. "It would do him good to get out among the *Youngie* and have fun."

After a moment, Malena said, "Do you think Cord minded that we were laughing at him this morning?"

Naomi wondered about the switch in subject from Alden to Cord. "If he did, you apologized."

"I felt bad. But I caught Alden's eye and it struck me so funny I couldn't help it. Alden does *not* want to teach Cord how to shoe a horse."

"Then if it comes up, he can tell him he doesn't want to."

"I'm tempted to make sure Cord's cowboy training is good and long, just so it's sure not to come up."

"More work for you, though," Naomi pointed out. "I don't see Rebecca and Sara volunteering to add to their list of chores, either."

"Dat said it was up to me and Zach," Malena said, resignation in her tone. Then she brightened. "But they'll be out in the hills tomorrow. Maybe I'll have some time to myself to work on a quilt."

"I hope so." Naomi judged it the right time to go inside and check on Deborah. Interesting that she'd gone out there to talk about Cord, and they'd spent half the time talking about Alden.

Very interesting indeed.

The following evening

Julie passed Alden a plate heaped with one of his favorites —something Mamm called Underground Ham Casserole. As a child, he'd eaten the layers one by one, starting with the ham and ending with the mashed potatoes. Now he was usually too hungry by dinnertime to be fussy.

"What's got under your skin? You're as restless as the chickens when they see a hawk."

Alden might not have called it *restless*, but he'd for sure and certain seen a hawk. And its name was Cord McLean. "Am I?" he said easily, taking a helping of salad, then passing the bowl of greens and tomatoes from the garden to their mother.

"Does it have something to do with the Circle M?" Julie helped herself to casserole and set the hot dish in the middle of the table.

"Julie, leave him alone," their mother said.

"Did you see that movie star?" Beth wanted to know.

"*Ja*, he was there. Seems he's going to be staying on the ranch for a week, to learn how to be a cowboy."

All three women lowered their forks to stare at him.

"Stay on the Circle M?" Mamm asked at last. "Reuben allowed it?"

"He might have changed his mind by now, but when I was there this morning, he did. Apparently Cord McLean's trainer got into a car accident, and the Rocking Diamond's trainer isn't available. He and Trey Madison rode over specifically to ask if Reuben and the boys could help."

"And Reuben said yes," Mamm said, as if checking that she'd heard correctly the first time.

"Naomi too." This was his favorite casserole, and yet the thought of that man sleeping in the same house as Malena made his appetite wither. "He talked them into it."

"Some talker," Julie observed. "Reuben Miller isn't the kind of man to be swayed once he's made up his mind that something is right or wrong."

That was the truth.

"I hope everything will be fine," Beth said. "This movie star—is he nice?"

"I guess." He still felt a little guilty about the whole family laughing, since he had a feeling he'd started it. But there had been that moment—just a sparkle of time when Malena had met his eye and they'd shared the humor in it—that he couldn't forget. It was the first time a moment had belonged to him and her, just themselves alone, before the family had joined in and the connection had been broken.

He wanted more moments like that. Would it be so bad to dream of strings of them—no, entire days made of such moments? And if it was possible, how could he make such a thing more than simply a dream?

"You guess." Beth's flat tone brought him back to the supper table and the subject at hand. "Does he smile? Is he polite? How is he going to manage the work?"

"*Ja, ja,* and I don't know," he told his sister. "Pass the bread, please."

She did, but now Julie jumped in. "Do you think he'll come to singing with them on Sunday?"

Now it was his turn to stare incredulously. "A worldly *Englisch* man, come to singing? Why would he want to?"

"I don't know. But if he did, then I could meet him."

"He's just a guy, Julie, like any other."

"Says you." She tilted her chin at him.

"Sunday is his day off. Reuben already told him he could go back to the Rocking Diamond. I'm sure the Madisons have so many ways to entertain him he won't need to add singing to the list."

"What about the auction?" Beth asked. "Is he going to that?"

What had got into his sisters? "How should I know? I was there to shoe two horses and we didn't speak."

"But you had coffee over there after," Julie said. "If they were talking about him staying, they'd have talked about the auction."

"Just that the family is going. That's it. Reuben said he could go or stay. There. You know what I know."

Julie exchanged a glance with her sister.

"You and a million other people will be trying to meet him," Alden added.

"I hope he does bring lots of people in," Mamm said, ever practical. "Good for us. Probably pretty inconvenient for him, though."

"I guess we'll have to see." Alden had had enough of Cord McLean. He took his empty plate to the sink. "I'm going over to the shop. The bishop brought over his flatbed wagon this afternoon. I want to make sure the gates are tied down good and proper before I take them to the Rocking Diamond tomorrow."

"Did they get the concrete poured for the posts?" Mamm asked.

He nodded. "Everything's ready. All I have to do is hang them."

One thing about the Madisons—they got things done. And woe betide you if you didn't come through on a promise yourself.

He had given himself the day off on Saturday. Both he and Mamm were closing up shop and spending the day at the auction, where for once in his adult life, he wasn't going to spend all his time checking out tools and supplies.

No, for the first time, he was going to a quilt auction.

Smiling at what Julie and Beth would probably have to say

about it, he ambled the three blocks back to the shop and let himself in. The smell of metal and horse and grease was as comforting to him as apple pie might be to other people. He checked the tiedowns on the gates, which lay wrapped in canvas on the bishop's flatbed, ready to be hitched up to Joseph in the morning.

They didn't really need checking—he had made certain everything was ready to go before he'd walked home for dinner. But he'd needed a little quiet time, and his shop was the best place for it.

Usually.

At the sound of his name, he turned to see Julie framed in the doorway, the light of the long northern evening behind her.

He couldn't remember the last time she'd had two minutes free to come visit the shop. *"Alles ischt okay?"* He straightened and crossed the concrete floor.

"Are you heading home?"

"Ja, I suppose."

"Okay if I walk with you?"

Ah. He got it now. She wanted to talk.

"Sure. What's up?"

He locked the door behind him and they strolled down the boardwalk, which ended about twenty feet on. The evening smelled of cut hay and dust, and from somewhere down in the creek that ran behind the shops on this side, a red-winged blackbird warbled its last song of the day.

"Nothing's up with me. I just wondered if everything was okay with you."

He didn't bother beating around the bush. "I don't like this *Englischer* at the Circle M, is all." He raised a hand. "I know. You don't need to say it. It's none of my business."

She smiled. "She's got her father and two *Brieder*, Alden. It's not like anything is going to happen to her."

He stopped, his boots scraping on the boardwalk. Then, without replying, he stepped off and waited for her to make the short jump, too.

"I'm right, aren't I?"

With a sigh, he gave in to the inevitable. Julie was the *Schweschder* he was closest to, and unfortunately for him sometimes, the one who was the most perceptive. "*Ja*. Not that it matters. Malena Miller doesn't know I'm alive, except as one of the *Youngie*. The person waiting to serve the volleyball. Someone in the food line."

Except for that moment of laughter. She had seen him then. But it hadn't lasted. Moments were like that. They happened, and then they were gone, no matter how much you wished them back.

"I wouldn't say that. I've seen you talking to her. She looked like she knew who she was with." He could hear the smile in her voice.

"She talks to everyone. And everyone wants to talk with her. Everyone wants to be with her. Cord McLean is probably no different."

"Even if he isn't, he's *Englisch*." She tilted her head to look up at him. "Is that the trouble? Alden, you know Malena Miller would no more get interested in an *Englischer* than fly to the moon."

"But I've seen the way he looks at her. She's so beautiful, of course he looks at her. What if he tries something?"

"Then she'll go to her father, and he'll toss him off the property."

"But it will have happened."

"Is that what's bothering you? The thought of Malena with

this movie star ... like that?"

He sighed. It sounded unsavory when she said it right out loud. Disloyal to Malena, somehow, as if he thought she didn't have any say in the matter. But she was an Amish girl. They didn't go around kissing people just for fun. Kisses were for the one God might have brought into your life. The one you hoped to marry.

Maybe she'd already kissed someone on a date. The very thought hurt him. Which was just him being a hypocrite, because he'd kissed a girl or two before. But those relationships hadn't gone anywhere. *Der Herr* had said no, and that was that.

"Alden? Did you hear me?"

"I heard you. And you're right, it bothers me to think of him there. With her. With the family."

"Because you wish it was you." Julie paused on the bridge over the creek, and the blackbird bobbed on a cattail, looking at them. Then, evidently deciding they weren't a threat, it sang again, a stave of liquid joy.

"Ja," he said in a low voice. "But you won't tell anyone."

"Of course not. What are you going to do?"

He lifted one shoulder in a shrug. "What can I do?"

"Something more than moping, to begin with. Watching her from afar is no way to make a girl take notice. Buy her something at the auction. An ice cream cone. A ticket to a drawing. I can ask if she'd like to go home from singing with you. Bontragers' is only a mile from the Circle M, so you won't have much time together in the buggy, but it's a start."

Love for his sister warmed his heart. "You would do that for me?"

"I'd do anything you asked me. Within *Gott's wille*," she added hastily, with a laugh.

This had to be *Gott's wille,* then. Julie wouldn't intrude into his nonexistent love life unless she'd been prompted by His still, small voice.

But her mind was still clearly picking at his problem, looking for a way to undo the knot. "You have to do something different to get her attention. Be something different."

"How can I be something different? I am what *der Herr* made me."

"He put endless potential into each of us," his sister said earnestly. "I don't mean change the way He made you. But look at yourself. There must be things inside you she would like to see and know. Thoughts she'd like to share. Things you could learn about yourself that she might like to learn, too."

How had Julie become so wise? "The way the *Englischer* is learning to be a cowboy?"

"Maybe he has that inside him. Maybe you have the husband for her inside you. You just have to let him out."

Maybe. And maybe he'd fall as flat as Cord McLean falling off his horse.

"It's like in those *Englisch* magazines at the checkout," Julie went on. "They call it a makeover. Everything about the person is the same, it's just arranged so that different aspects of them show better. You can do that—I know you can."

He wasn't so sure. But even so, he began turning ideas over in his mind as he and Julie walked home in a companionable silence. He couldn't see how he could pull off one of them just yet, but the thought wouldn't leave him.

What if he won the bid for Malena's Glacier Lily quilt?

Would she see that as the action of a man who cared? Would it show her for sure and certain that the man who respected her gifts and cared for her most was right here in front of her?

Friday morning

ALDEN BROUGHT Joseph to a halt in the drive of the Rocking Diamond promptly at seven o'clock. As he was untying the ropes around the gates and releasing the canvas tarps, he heard the sound of small engines. In a moment, two four-wheelers burst around the curve, Chance Madison on one and his youngest brother Clint on the other. The machines growled to a stop on the far side of the existing gate and his customer's sons hopped off.

"Saw you coming," Chance said by way of greeting. "Need a hand?"

"That'd be great. These gates are heavy."

The three of them unloaded the wrought-iron gates made to Brock Madison's design. In the center of each half was their brand, a diamond on point with a short curve like a rocker under it. Bars of iron, laboriously twisted one at a time, radiated out from the diamond like the rays of the sun, and across the top like a banner were the words *Rocking Diamond Ranch* in a wrought script that had taken him longer than all the rest of the construction put together.

The uprights slid into their new closures without a hitch, and Alden saw that an intercom system had been installed as well. The eye of a camera regarded him solemnly from the top of the concrete and brick post.

"Dad's happy you got them done on time." Clint tended to say whatever crossed his mind. Most of the time Alden appreciated it, but sometimes the young man's thoughts weren't as kind as they could be. But he supposed that was the Madisons' problem, not his.

"I am, too. Can you let your dad know Doc MacDonald and I were thinking about next week to shoe the second string? He wanted to get that done before roundup."

"Will do," Chance said easily. He dug in his pocket and pulled out an envelope. "Here's the balance."

Alden took it and counted the cash. All present and accounted for. Almost. "It's twenty dollars short."

Clint grinned. "Consider it the cost of our labor."

Something tightened in Alden's chest. "My agreement was with your dad. Does he know you took your tip out of his money?"

Clint hooked his thumbs in his leather belt and rocked back on his heels. "I don't bother Dad with small stuff."

Alden nodded. And seeing an artisan correctly paid was small stuff. Since the *Ordnung* said their shirts weren't to have pockets, and his broadfall pants didn't, he pulled up one pant leg and slid the envelope into his boot. "I'll send him an invoice."

"For twenty bucks?" Clint looked as if this was the stupidest thing he'd ever heard. "You Amish are so cheap you squeak."

Turn the other cheek. His mother's voice sounded in his head, saying the words they all knew. *If a man asks for your coat, give him your cloak also.*

"Your dad's a businessman," Alden said mildly. "He believes in full payment of his debts. What will he say when he finds out you shorted me and took that money yourself?"

"That he made a mistake," Clint said. "It happens. Miscounted. Can't prove I took it, can you?" When Alden said nothing, the young man flushed. "What are you going to do? Shake me down?"

He was spoiling for a fight. In Alden's experience, shame at their poor choices being exposed made people angry. The only thing they wanted to do was take it out on the guy who made them feel that way. And Alden knew better than to play that game.

Silently, he turned away and began to fold the canvas tarps. When he had them in a neat pile, he tied them down to the bed of the wagon. When he reached up to get in, Chance said, "Thought you might come up to the house for something to eat. Maria's making breakfast burritos before she starts on the guests' food."

"No, thanks." Alden picked up the reins. "You can tell your dad I've remembered another job next week. MacDonald will have to shoe those horses on his own."

"Hey," Chance protested. "Don't be mad. My brother was just joking around."

"That twenty dollars was going toward horseshoes. Now I don't have enough for your job. Maybe it's a joke to Clint, there, but it won't be very funny to Doc MacDonald. It's his busiest time of year, with everyone wanting shoes before roundup."

Clint swore with violence and quite a bit of imagination

before stomping over and throwing the twenty at Alden's head. Calmly, Alden picked it up off the floor of the wagon and slid it into his boot. Then he shook the reins over Joseph's back and they lurched into motion.

He didn't look back to see the four-wheelers hightailing it up the lane. He could hear them well enough.

"What do you think about that, Joseph?"

The horse twitched an ear in his direction, then focused on the road ahead.

"I agree with you. Best to keep quiet and not mention this to his father. I'll do as scripture says, and pray for that kid."

Which he did, all the way to the bishop's barn, where he and Joseph backed the wagon into its place.

The bishop walked in through the open barn doors as he was unhitching. "Alden. I thought it was you. Everything go all right with the gates?"

"*Ja,*" he said easily. "If the Madisons wanted the lane up to their place to be noticed, they got their wish. I never made such gaudy gates before. Lucky for me, cows prefer plain bars."

"Maybe the Madisons don't want all those newspaper reporters getting lost." The bishop grinned. "Say, are you going by the Circle M? Ruby made a list of all the quilts up for auction, with the name of the quilter and where it was from. She photocopied them at the post office so Malena's helpers could hand them out at the door."

"Good idea," Alden said, trying for a casual note in his voice. He hoped the bishop hadn't noticed his heart taking off at a gallop.

"Seems they do this for the bidders at the Rexford auction. Ruby's putting up about a hundred quarts of tomato sauce this morning and won't be able to get over there. Do you have the time?"

He might have a list of jobs as long as his arm, but he put that one at the top of it without a moment's hesitation. "Sure. I'll buckle up Joseph's tack while you get it."

When Little Joe came back, he had a fat manila envelope in one hand and an apple turnover in the other. "Ruby says *denki*."

"It's me who should be saying that." The turnover smelled like cider and the pastry crust melted in his mouth. "This is *gut*."

When he finished it, he mounted Joseph from a fence rail and rode him out of the barn, the envelope tucked securely under his arm.

"*Der Herr* is making some kind of a point," he told Joseph a few minutes later, as they turned into the lane belonging to the Circle M. "That's twice in three days I've had to come over here. Do you think He's trying to tell me something?"

But Joseph, smart horse that he was, wouldn't commit himself one way or the other.

❧

REBECCA LEANED INTO MALENA'S ROOM AS SHE WAS MULLING over the arrangement of squares and diamonds that could form a design on two levels for Joshua and Sara's wedding quilt. They planned to marry on October 12, and live permanently at the hay farm. Sara was already at work making favors and hand-writing invitations.

"Alden is here, riding bareback," Becca said. "Looks like he has a parcel of some kind for us."

It wasn't likely it was for her, and it was too early for the mail, but all the same, a person should be polite when a guest came to the door. Malena followed her twin out on the deck just in time to see Alden swing down from the horse that usually pulled the farrier's wagon. It was rare to see an Amish person riding bareback in their district—and on that big horse, it was a long way to the ground.

Alden saw her and held up the parcel in lieu of a wave. "*Guder mariye.* I dropped off the bishop's flatbed wagon and he asked if I'd bring this over. Ruby sent it for you." After he tied the Belgian to the rail, he loped up the stairs to join them.

Malena took the packet with a smile and peeked in. "The lot list for the quilt auction."

"What number are you?" Rebecca asked.

Malena scanned the double-sided list. "Six. Oh good. If I'd had to wait until twenty-two I'd have combusted from sheer nerves."

"Is twenty-two the last one? Who is it?" Alden leaned in to look.

"One of the Lapps from St Ignatius." She slid a photocopy out of the envelope. "Want one?"

"Sure." Before she could react, he took it from her with a smile.

"You're going to bid on a quilt?" came out of her mouth before she could stop it.

"I never have before, but someone tells me every year what I missed not going. I hear it gets pretty exciting. Not like pallets of iron stock."

Someone? One of his sisters, maybe. Speaking of sisters, Rebecca had disappeared, probably to put the coffee on and take some butter tarts out of the cooling cupboard.

Alden was still looking at the lot list. "Do all the quilts have names?"

"Not all. If they don't, Ruby and I give them a name so we

can keep the lots straight. *Log cabin with brown-and-white border and coffee pots in the center squares* doesn't fit in the first column."

With a laugh, he nodded. "*Coffee Pots* is short and snappy, all right. *Earth and Stars.* What's that one?"

"You should see it. A quilter from Rexford made it and sent it down with her son-in-law. It's a big star, but each of the points is pieced to look like a mountain, from forest at the base to slopes to white peaks. And there are acorns and oak leaves quilted in the borders. I'm thinking it will fetch a nice price. Her quilts usually do."

"Not as much as *Glacier Lily.*" His gaze met hers, and color crept into his face.

She fussed with the knot in the back of her kitchen apron. "Your mamm thinks it might fetch a bit. I hope it does. Our scholars need a couple of rows of new desks."

A little silence fell.

Then he folded the list and slipped it into his boot. "Well, I'd best be going. Now that the Rocking Diamond's gates are installed, I can catch up on a week's worth of work."

"*Neh*, don't go," she said. He'd been here less than ten minutes. "Becca's probably got the coffee on. And we can finish the butter tarts before Josh gets back from the farm."

"That's a hard one to turn down, but..." His smile wasn't the kind that said yes. "Tell you what. I'll take a rain check and buy you an ice cream cone tomorrow instead."

Luckily there was a rail under her elbow, or she might have fallen off the deck in sheer surprise. A dozen responses—jokes —ribbing—flashed through her brain, but what came out was, "I hope it doesn't rain."

Which was the most lame thing ever.

The light went out of his face. "Does that mean no?"

"*Neh*, it was just me being silly," she said hastily. "I'd love an ice cream cone. The Yoder boys make it right there behind the snack tent. I heard a rumor it's strawberry cheesecake this year."

The light had come back into his eyes. His hazel eyes. How had she never noticed what color his eyes were before?

"I've never had a chance to try it," he admitted. "I figured that two dollars was better spent on stock and equipment. Until now."

"Time for a change." She pulled herself together and smiled. The kind that *did* mean yes.

He blinked, as though the sun had come out from behind a cloud and dazzled him.

"*Ja*. Well. See you tomorrow," he said after a moment, and loped down the stairs.

Minutes later, she was still standing on the deck, waiting to see if he would look back and wave when he passed through the gap in the trees. Rebecca came out the kitchen door carrying a tray with three mugs of coffee and a plate of butter tarts.

"Is he gone? Why didn't he stay for coffee?" She put the tray down on the picnic table that lived there year round.

"He has work to do, I guess."

There he was. And sure enough, he lifted a hand as he rode the Belgian into the gap. Malena waved back, and then he was past, and the pines blocked him from view.

"He's going to buy me an ice cream cone tomorrow."

Rebecca's gaze swung abruptly from the view to Malena's face. Unaccountably, she could feel heat prickling in her cheeks.

"You're blushing." Her sister's voice was soft with discovery, as though she'd never seen such a thing before.

"I am not." But controlling a blush was every bit as impossible as controlling a giggle in church.

Malena expected Rebecca to give her a hard time about it. But it seemed her sister had learned a thing or two during her courtship with Noah. She simply handed Malena a mug of hot coffee, and they both took a succulent tart, then resumed their places at the rail.

"Have you heard from Noah?" He was due back any day.

"*Ja*, sort of." Rebecca chuckled. "I ran into Susan at the café when I was getting some things for the babies this morning. Simeon had just called to say they were at the train station in Denver. They should be here tonight."

Rebecca couldn't hide the excitement in her voice.

"I'm surprised you can be so calm, *Liewi*. I'd be bouncing off the walls if my special friend was coming back after three months away."

"We've been writing a couple of times a week."

"You know what I mean. Who is meeting them in Libby?" The train got in at midnight, so buggies were out of the question.

"Arlon and Kate King hired an *Englisch* taxi to collect them. The folks who bought Sim and Noah's house in Amity are sending their equipment and the furniture by freight later on."

"Furniture for a house?" Malena asked innocently.

"Ha ha, very funny." But Becca couldn't keep the smile off her lips. "I hope Susan likes it."

"Susan would like plywood laid on apple boxes if Simeon provided it for her. Do you think they have an understanding?"

"How could they not? She's stuck to him like honey when he's in town, and he seems to like it." Rebecca shook her head. Susan Bontrager was an acquired taste, but if *der Herr* meant her for Simeon King's wife, Malena hoped they would be very happy.

"I guess we just have to wait until Little Joe announces it in church," Malena said at last. "Meanwhile, I'm way more interested in Noah's plans. I'm thinking he'll take you to the auction and pop the question over the flower baskets."

Rebecca laughed. "It's a little soon for that. We only met in April, and he's been gone since May."

"You know what Dat says. Sometimes love isn't a matter of length, but depth. And goodness knows you two have gone through enough to make that true."

Rebecca nodded. "I wonder when it will be your turn, *Schweschder* of mine?"

"Whenever *Gott* decides it will be." She did not follow Rebecca's gaze back down the lane to the gap in the pines.

By tomorrow, Alden would probably have forgotten about the ice cream, so she'd pretend she had, too. She was going to be too busy to worry about it, anyway. The hanging line for the quilts was already strung between two poles, but it was up to her and one of her helpers to get the first two quilts up for bid on the line, and keep the colorful, neatly folded quilts in their plastic bags organized and ready to move onto the line before the auctioneer called them. Her other helper would stand at the door to hand out the lot lists, and a third would write up the winner's paper, which they'd take to Sadie in the cashier's booth. It was a brisk and noisy and wonderful process, and she could hardly wait for tomorrow.

In spite of herself, her gaze slid toward the gap in the trees.

But of course it was empty.

❧ 7 ❧

MOUNTAIN HOME AMISH SCHOOL

Saturday morning, 6:55 a.m.

WHEN MALENA and Ruby Wengerd drove into the schoolyard, their buggy packed to the ceiling with quilts neatly wrapped in plastic dry-cleaning bags, she saw that *Englisch* vehicles were already parked in the softball field. The boys who were in charge of parking—both buggies and cars— had marked the aisles neatly with orange baling string on sticks. A sign with BUGGIES handwritten on it directed the Amish visitors to the parking area closest to the bishop's pasture on the far side, where the horses could be unhitched. This was a Yoder innovation, to keep chaos from breaking out as people arrived and departed, and spare the horses' nerves.

Malena drove around to the back of the quilt tent. Their first task was to put the folded, wrapped quilts in order and later, to peg the first two up on the heavy line that would display them. The line had to be high enough to display the quilts at full length, while low enough for someone to reach it.

The Yoders had promised three stepladders for her and her helpers.

The quilts weren't heavy, of course, but folded into roughly the same dimensions, they certainly were bulky. It took a fair amount of time to get them arranged in order on the long table behind the display line, with a square of orange paper pinned to each one showing the same information as the lot list.

"Twenty-two quilts," Ruby said, gazing up at the empty line with its sturdy clothes pegs. "That means we only have to climb up there eleven times, *ja*?"

"Don't the *Englisch* buy machines that make you climb stairs?" Malena asked whimsically. "We get the same benefit for free."

"Those are called stair-steppers," said a male voice from the tent door. "What are you climbing on?"

Malena and Ruby both turned to see Trey Madison standing in the doorway. Cord McLean let the flap fall behind them and strolled inside. Good grief. The day hadn't even begun and here was the first distraction.

"We're not open yet," she said in her best cheerful tone. "Viewing is at ten, and the auction begins at eleven."

"We came for the guided tour," Cord said. "But if you need help, we're your men."

Did his emphasis on those last words have some kind of double meaning? "I thought you had chores this morning."

"I did. Finished them. Or at least, Zach said he'd finish them for me. There wasn't much left to do—just washing the buggies before the family comes over."

Dat couldn't exactly force a man to do chores. Malena had found out from Zach that the movie star was paying them two hundred dollars a day for the privilege, including room and board. If he wanted to pay and not do the work that would train him for his movie, she supposed that was up to him.

"Thanks, but we don't need help," Ruby said in her gentle voice. Malena knew it was an effort for her to speak up to someone who wasn't Amish, which made her appreciate her friend even more.

Cord and Trey didn't seem to hear. They strolled up to the display table and Cord said, "Which one did you make, Malena?"

"Lot six." Couldn't they take a hint?

He laid a hand on it. "This one? Nice." They had folded it so that part of the Glacier Lily wreath showed, and enough of the background piecing to give the prospective buyer an idea of how it might look once hung. "I'm going to bid on it."

She did her best to control her face. Her beautiful Glacier Lily, being snatched away by this careless man? Zach had said he'd been game enough to mend fences yesterday, but by the end of the day he'd been cutting wire short and dropping tools. Ranch work was tiring, she knew, but surely he could have admitted he was ready to ride in, and done something less destructive in the barn? What would happen to her quilt in his care?

"I hope you brought your wallet," was all she said. "Cash only."

"You don't take credit cards?"

She gave him a *really?* sort of look. "Do you see electricity in here?"

His gaze bounced around the tent as though, despite his experience with lamps and propane lately, it had never occurred to him. Then he said to Trey in an urgent tone, "Tell me there's an ATM in town."

"There's an ATM in town, but only one. There should still

be money in it at this time of day."

"The ATM *runs out of money?*"

You'd think he'd just been told that bank robbers rode in every morning and looted it.

"Come on," Cord commanded, already walking to the door. "We can hang out with the ladies later."

And then, thank goodness, they were gone.

Ruby made a choking noise.

"Are you two all right?" Dave put down the stepladders he carried. He asked the question of both, but his eyes were all for Ruby. His brother set up the third ladder next to the far pole and wasted no time in jostling Dave out of the way.

"Glad to see you enjoying yourself, Ruby," Cal said. "Maybe I could buy you an ice cream later?"

Malena had to get hold of herself. She was supposed to be organizing this auction, not laughing like a woodpecker. Besides, she needed to save her poor friend from these two. "Put one of those in the middle, if you could, and the other at this end."

Rebecca arrived a minute later, along with Susan Bontrager. Both were glowing—and Malena didn't even have to ask why. The two reasons for it lifted the tent flap and stepped inside after them.

"Hallo, Simeon, welcome back. It's good to see you, Noah," she said. She felt free to hug her sister's special friend, but Simeon wasn't the kind of man you just spontaneously hugged. He was the eldest of the three King brothers, a serious man with firm views about things. But this was balanced by a talent for making a success of their carpentry business. She'd leave the hugging to Susan if their courtship progressed that far.

"We weren't expecting to see you so early," Ruby said. "Not if the train got in at midnight."

"If losing a little sleep is the price to pay to see my friends sooner, I'll do it." Noah smiled down at Rebecca, who snuggled against his side with such contentment and happiness in her pretty face that Malena felt a tug of loss at her own heart.

But how could she feel the loss of something she'd never experienced? Not seriously, anyway. Driving home with a boy from singing and his clumsy attempts to steal a kiss were not this. She'd never once floated into the house with the certain knowledge that she had just said good night to *der Herr*'s choice for her.

She'd hazard a guess that Noah wouldn't wait until the flower wagons were loaded with baskets of blossoms, or even for the full moon next week to create a romantic moment. He looked like he wanted to propose that very second.

"Can we offer you a hand?" Susan said, seemingly unaware of what was transpiring right beside her. "Is everything ready?"

"*Ja,*" Malena replied, waving a hand over the table as if presenting that year's quilts to an enthusiastic audience. "We have a while before viewing starts. Want to walk around and see the rest of the auction?"

"I do," Rebecca said, so of course Noah agreed.

"We have all day," Susan objected.

"I'd like a look at some of the furniture before the bidding starts," Simeon said. "Ours is coming in a couple of weeks, but we could use a few pieces."

"All right," Susan said instantly. "I'd like a bookcase, and I hear the Zook brothers are going to offer a new flavor of cheese in the food displays in the schoolhouse. Their dilly goat cheese omelette is the second most popular item on our breakfast menu—I don't know how they can top it."

The two of them wandered off without waiting for anyone to join them—which was probably just as well. Malena's gaze met that of her twin and found a twinkle there that told her she was thinking the same thing.

She linked her arm with Ruby's. "Let's have a look around. And if I see something I absolutely must have, you're to march me back here right away."

They tied the tent door shut and made sure the sign indicating the viewing and auction times hung straight, and headed off for the furniture tent. Handmade furniture came from all over the country to the school auctions in the west, but for this one, it was *wunderbaar* how many items had been handmade by Amish craftsmen right here in the Siksika.

Noah and Rebecca drifted off. Malena didn't have the heart to elbow in on their first day together by insisting that they stay a foursome. Besides, Ruby was good company once you got her talking—and once they discouraged the valley's young men. Did these boys not realize that the bishop's daughter was not a prize trout, ready for the first one to catch her? She was a person with her own thoughts and feelings—and worth a more gentle approach to get to know her.

Malena had learned long ago that being the bishop's daughter was no easy thing. Everyone in the church watching you to make sure your example was perfect. No wonder she hardly spoke when every word was weighed and measured.

Zach ambled up to join them, at which point Ruby closed up like a clam, too shy to get out another sentence.

"Finished washing the buggies, did you?" Malena asked her brother pleasantly.

"Didn't take long, even if my helper ran out on me."

"Oh? I heard you offered."

"It doesn't matter," he said easily. "It was only the one, for Mamm and Sara and the *Bopplin*. Josh and I walked over with Daniel and his family."

"It's funny to think of Daniel with a family," Malena said. "At this time last year, he and Lovina hadn't even met ... again."

"And now, he's got both a wife and a son," Ruby managed to add.

"I hope their family grows," Malena said. "Imagine, three *Bopplin* on the Circle M, all born within a year of one another. Daniel's Joel will have his hands full with cousins."

"And loving every minute," Zach said with a laugh. "Are you two looking for anything special?"

"I wanted to see if there was a sewing table," Malena replied. "Ruby, remember the one last year, with the expansion that slid out and all the cubbyholes?"

"I remember the price tag on it," Ruby said. "Maybe the carpenter has made another one for this year."

Zach must not have anything else to do, or else the Yoder boys were busy, Malena thought as they walked up and down the three aisles of bedroom sets, dining room sets, coffee tables, and bookcases. And then she forgot about everything but the fact that a table almost like last year's was once again on display.

She covered her eyes. "Ruby, tell me quickly. How much are they asking?"

Her friend whispered the number in her ear and Malena groaned. "I guess I'd better get some more quilts into Rose's shop if I want to afford that."

"You've got your cattle money, haven't you?" Zach asked.

"Imagine Dat's face if I told him I spent it on a sewing table. *Neh*, Mamm's is good enough for me." She sighed, and turned her back on the lovely thing. "I will stand firm and go back to the quilt tent where I belong."

"I want to look around a little longer," Ruby said. "But I'll be there well in time for viewing."

Malena left them to themselves. Zach was as quiet a person as Ruby. She hoped they'd have a wonderful time saying nothing to each other while they looked at the beautiful hand-made items ready to be auctioned.

The quilt auction tent was exactly as they'd left it. She walked slowly to the head of the display table. To hang the first two for the viewing, or not? She was ruminating when she heard the whisper of canvas and turned.

Oh.

"Hey." Cord McLean walked over with an easy stride, hands in his jeans pockets.

"Did you find the ATM?"

He slapped his hip pocket. "It took me three credit cards to get the amount I wanted, but I got it. I hope nobody picks my pocket. They'll be rich."

"Here?" She raised an eyebrow. "Not likely."

"Good to know. What are you doing?"

Wishing you'd go away and leave me to think. But *neh*, she couldn't say that out loud. She'd offend him, and he might leave before the week was up, and the Circle M would lose the unexpected windfall that could help with expenses. Since this year's calves wouldn't be sold until after roundup, every dollar counted just now.

So she said, "I'm trying to decide whether I should hang the first two quilts or not. Viewing opens at ten."

"Why shouldn't you?" He walked to the head of the table and looked the first two over.

"Because it might give them an unfair advantage. None of the others are displayed."

"You should hang the one you made."

She snorted. "My first year in charge of the auction, and I display my own quilt? That would be the very definition of prideful. Our bishop's wife would never let me help again, and she'd be right not to."

"Prideful?" He looked honestly puzzled. "Seems to me it's more like a benefit. A perk for all the work you've put in."

"There are many others who have put in just as much work," she told him. "If everyone pushed and shoved to give their things the best place, imagine what chaos this whole auction would turn into."

He laughed. "I guess you're right."

She supposed she couldn't blame him for not knowing how to look at life the Amish way. "We believe in giving place, not taking place. That way, everyone gets a place."

"If you say so. But in my world, if I did that, I'd disappear in the crowd."

To an Amish person, that was the point. Mammi had cross-stitched a bookmark for her years ago that said, *It takes the effort of every blade of grass to keep the meadow green.* When you looked at a meadow, you saw its beauty. Not individual blades of grass.

"Oh, I don't think you would," she said without thinking.

She hadn't meant anything by it. But he seemed to take it as a compliment. Worse, as encouragement. And here he was, crowding her as she stood at the head of the long table. As if there wasn't twelve or fifteen feet for him to take up space in.

"Now, what did you mean by that?" he said in a caressing tone.

"Nothing." She took a step to one side. The tent was beginning to feel a little stuffy. The canvas became almost translucent as the sun rose over the treetops outside.

He took a step, too. "Did you mean ... you think I stand out in a crowd?"

"I don't know, Cord." Another step away. "Why don't you go outside and see?"

"I can't. A news van pulled up five minutes ago. I'm actually in here hiding."

Of course he assumed they were there to put *him* on the news, not the auction, which would be attended by a thousand people if everything went well. She looked him in the eye. "You. Hiding from a camera. Do you know where liars go?"

"To Washington?"

What? She frowned at him.

"Ma-lay-na," he crooned. "Don't spoil your pretty face like that. You'll make me not want to kiss you."

"That would probably be best," said a voice from the door.

॰॰॰

THE TWO OF THEM JUMPED APART AS ALDEN TIED THE TENT door open. He felt sick to his stomach—they had been standing so close, saying goodness knew what, until she'd made a face at him and he'd said that about not kissing her. How had it progressed so far in just a couple of days? Cord McLean was playing with her, anybody could see that. But Alden had no right to say any more than he already had—and that was being plenty forward as it was. Elbowing his way into a brother's place when he most certainly did not want her to think of him as a brother.

Malena Miller could take care of herself. But all the same, she was out of her league with this worldly *Englischer*.

"It's quarter to ten," Alden said mildly. "Anything I can do before the folks start coming in?"

Her cheeks flew scarlet flags of emotion—embarrassment or temper at his interference, he couldn't tell. But her voice was steady. *"Neh, denki."* Was she speaking *Deitsch* deliberately, to exclude Cord? And was that a subtle stress on *denki?* As though she was glad he'd come in just then?

He must be imagining it. She'd refused his help, no more.

He was turning to leave them alone, when Malena said, "Wait—the Yoder girls were supposed to be here by now to hand out lot lists to people." She hurried over to a side table and slid half the sheets out of the envelope he'd brought over to the Circle M yesterday. "Can you stand by the door and give these out?"

He'd lie down in a creek if she wanted to cross it on his back. "Sure."

Her face flushed again. "I mean, I know you probably have more important things to do, but—"

Over her shoulder he could see Cord lounging against one of the display line poles, watching them. He made up his mind.

"We're all here to support the auction. If that helps it make as much money as possible, I'll do it."

"Denki," she said again. "We'll be done by noon, and then you can have your day back."

"Ischt okay," he assured her. "I've already done my business. Got a nice lot of bar stock and a drill press. That was a real find. Glad I brought Joseph to haul it home—it weighs two hundred pounds."

The color in her cheeks was fading, leaving her skin its usual soft peaches and cream. "I'm so pleased you got it," she told him. "I hope you won't—"

But whatever she'd meant to say was cut off by the arrival of a gabbling flock of reporters, who had clearly been tipped off to the movie star's whereabouts. People outside must have heard the ruckus, because they began streaming into the tent to see what was going on, ignoring Alden and the lot lists, making a beeline for the cameras, their own cell phones already out to take Cord's picture.

"The quilts!" Malena said urgently, and hurried over to the table, which was in danger of being upset by the pushing crowd. "Cord, for goodness sake, can you take these people outside?"

"I'm bringing your bidders in," he called. "You should be thanking me."

"Who's this?" one of the reporters said. "You know these Amish people?"

Alden lunged as the huge camera on the man's shoulder swung on Malena. He got his back in front of it just in time to prevent her being filmed, giving her two precious seconds to turn her own back. "We don't allow pictures," he said firmly. "Please turn it away."

"Why not?" the man asked, lowering his camera. "Just walking over here from the road, I got all kinds of shots of your people."

"Children, maybe, or people at a distance or with their backs turned," Alden said. "Nothing where you could identify the person. A photograph is a graven image to us, and the Bible forbids those."

"No kidding." The man sounded mystified, but at least he didn't put up an argument.

"Come on, Matt," the man with him urged. "Cord's going to give us an interview."

"Not in here, please," Alden said, trying to get the movie star's attention, to no avail.

The knot around Cord was a babble of people trying to get closer while the reporters rattled off questions.

"Look this way, Mr McLean."

"How is cowboy training going?"

"Please, Cord, can we get a selfie with you?" This was from a bunch of *Englisch* girls in cut-off shorts and tank tops.

"Wow," Malena said. "Do you think he actually likes this?"

"Hard to tell." But in Alden's mind, he sure seemed to. He answered every single question, smiled for the camera, and took picture after picture with the girls and anyone else who asked him. In any other situation, the excitement would have worn off once people had the pictures they wanted. But here, the crowd only seemed to grow, both in size and in volume.

Two Amishmen came in the door and stopped short, trying to figure out if it was a crisis or whether someone was hurt. At this rate, somebody *was* going to get overexcited and need an EMT.

Malena groaned. "It's the auctioneers—I have to speak to them. Alden, can you keep these *Englisch* away from the front? I'm afraid someone is going to tip over the table."

"Of course." He handed her the lot lists and took up a position where he could grab the table if the crowd surged this way.

Malena greeted the auctioneers and asked them if they'd had a good trip from Indiana. Alden knew that being an auctioneer was a special skill, and men with that skill traveled all over the country for events like this. For smaller events, too, like selling off the furniture and equipment of a farm after the passing of its owners.

Malena brought them over and introduced them as Rodney Beachy and Seth Eicher. "We're going to need a fellow to encourage the crowd to bid," Rodney, the senior man, said to Alden. "Any chance you might help?"

This was miles out of Alden's league. "I've never even been to a quilt auction," he said. "What would I have to do?"

"You've probably seen them in the equipment tent," Seth

said. He was about Alden's age. "You wave your hands like this —" He demonstrated a *come on* motion. "—and help us spot people who have raised their hands but not enough to see. And maybe one or two are undecided and you can encourage them to bid. Answer questions if you're able. Can you do that?"

"I—well, I—" How was he supposed to convince someone to bid if they hadn't already decided on it? Or answer questions about quilts? The only quilt he knew anything about was the Glacier Lily.

"Please, Alden," Malena begged. "I need all the help in here I can get."

That decided him. "All right."

The Yoder girls burst through the tent door and ran up in a flurry of apologies and questions. And then, to Alden's surprise, at least half of the people in Cord's admiring crowd decided to find chairs for the quilt auction. Lot lists were given out and now a crowd formed around the display tables. With a sense of relief, he saw Cord take the reporters outside, which made the noise level drop significantly.

It seemed like no time before Malena and Ruby carefully stripped the flimsy plastic off the first two quilts and advanced together to the display line. They climbed the stepladders in unison and pegged up the two quilts.

Alden took up a position where he could see as much of his half of the tent as he could, while Seth took the far side. Rodney Beachy mounted the small stage and took his place at the auctioneer's lectern. "Welcome, welcome, folks, to the Mountain Home Amish School quilt auction," he said in a booming voice that needed no microphone. "We hope you've had a look over the beautiful quilts you'll be bidding on today. If you haven't got a lot list, just wave a hand and we'll see that you get one. Up first is Coffee Pots. Who's going to start the bidding at fifty dollars? Do I have fifty dollars? Thank you. A hundred dollars—yes, there we are ..."

In about two minutes the bidding was up to eight hundred dollars, and Alden could only stand there in admiration of the auctioneer's skill, to say nothing of how fast his mouth could move.

"Sold!" Rodney cried in triumph at eight hundred fifty, and Coffee Pots was removed from the line. The second quilt was moved into its place by Malena and Ruby, and the Yoder sisters unwrapped a third to peg up for people to appreciate before bidding began on it.

The bidding sped to its conclusion five more times, the quilts made their way on and off the display line, and Alden's heart kicked into a brisk trot as Glacier Lily was moved from the display position to active bidding. A murmur rippled through the crowd loudly enough for Rodney to hear.

"Isn't this a beauty?" he asked with a big smile. "Who wouldn't want Glacier Lily in their home? I think we'd better start the bidding at two hundred dollars, hey? Who will give two hundred dollars for this one-of-a-kind quilt?"

Alden's hand shot into the air of its own volition.

At the front of the room, standing ready near the middle stepladder, Malena's mouth fell into an *O* the same shape as her wide eyes.

"We have two hundred. Who will give me three hundred for this quilt, handmade right here in the Siksika Valley?"

The bidding shot up—and up. Alden saw the inevitability of its going for a thousand dollars barreling down on him like an Amtrak train, and could hardly concentrate enough to bring a woman in the back wearing a green windbreaker to Rodney's attention.

"A thousand dollars!" Rodney cried, clearly enjoying himself. "Who will be brave enough to bid a thousand for this unique and practical work of art?"

Alden's hand flew into the air and Malena's face went stark white.

"Eleven hundred! Do I have eleven hundred, ladies and gentlemen. Thank you, there in the back in the green jacket. Do I have twelve hundred?"

Twelve hundred. What was he thinking? He couldn't possibly.

Alden's hand went up.

"Twelve hundred, thank you! Who will give me thirteen hundred?"

Alden felt like he was going to faint. His hand trembled. Twitched. Wavered.

"Thirteen hundred, thank you to the man in the granite Resistol. Do I have fourteen hundred?"

The granite Resistol?

Alden's hand flew into the air.

"Fourteen hundred, thank you very much, do I hear fifteen? Yes indeed, we have fifteen hundred. Fifteen hundred, do I hear sixteen?"

Alden turned to glare at Cord McLean, standing there at the back of the crowd in his granite-colored Resistol hat, looking the part of a cowboy. The camera was still on him as he bid.

"Do I hear sixteen?"

Alden's hand rose halfway.

"Sixteen hundred, do I hear seventeen hund—thank you, that Resistol makes you real easy to see. Not to mention the camera. Do I hear eighteen hundred?"

Eighteen hundred was more than Alden made in a month.

He couldn't do this. He couldn't. Both his sisters and his mother were sitting halfway back, staring at him in complete dismay. How were they going to pay the rent if he bid on—

"Seventeen hundred going once."

Alden pushed his hand into the air as though it were plowing through mud.

"Eighteen hundred! Nineteen hundred, thank you, lady in the green jacket. Do I hear two thousand? An even two thousand. Highest bid ever at the Mountain Home Amish School quilt auction. Come, folks, set a record. Do I hear two thousand?"

Alden's mind reeled. He couldn't breathe properly.

"Two thousand!" Rodney crowed in triumph. "Do I hear twenty-one? No bids at twenty-one? Going once at two thousand. Going twice. *Sold* to the young man in the granite Resistol. I hope the lady you plan to give it to appreciates how much you love her. Next up is the ..."

But Alden never heard the name of the next quilt. A roaring sounded in his ears as the world swung around him. As he watched Malena, moving stiffly, take Glacier Lily down off the line, fold it carefully, and hold it against her chest while Ruby slipped the dry-cleaning bag over it once more. They marked the bidder's name on the orange slip and while the Yoder girls moved the next quilt up the line, Ruby made her way around the rows of benches to give the slip to Cord. He would take it to the cashier's booth, hand over his two thousand dollars, and get a receipt.

Once he handed Sadie's proof of payment to Malena, he would leave with the quilt.

And some part of Malena's heart, for sure and certain, would go out the door with it.

✢ 8 ✢

ALDEN WAS NOT ABOUT to wait around to see certainty become reality. He grabbed David Yoder, who was holding up a tent wall close by, probably watching over his sisters. He explained in a rapid undertone what to do. When Dave obligingly agreed to be Seth and Rodney's "encourager," he fled the quilt auction as fast as he could.

He had to find somewhere to be alone. To breathe. To recover from the most stressful ten minutes of his life, with a crashing disappointment bringing up the rear like the stinger in a scorpion's tail.

Going into the schoolhouse, full of food displays and likely a good percentage of the church district's women, was out of the question. The furniture tent was a possibility, especially now that he hadn't blown a month's income on a quilt. But in the end there was nothing quite as comforting as the neat stacks of used parts and farm equipment, set in orderly piles in the level lot behind the schoolhouse where, in winter, the scholars banked up snow to make a hockey rink.

It took a good fifteen minutes for the shaking in his hands

to calm. And for him to recognize that his dizziness was probably the result of his breakfast wearing off.

He didn't know how to explain his hot, red face. The closest he could come was grief.

Over being outbid on a quilt.

He could have handled it better if it had been the lady in the green windbreaker. But to lose Malena's beautiful quilt to Cord McLean? To lose what was probably his best opportunity to show her he cared?

Head down, thankful for the brim of his straw hat, he closed his eyes and struggled to keep the tears at bay.

"Alden? *Bischt du okay?*"

The familiar voice of Zach Miller forced his eyes open. His friend had ambled up right beside him and Alden hadn't even been aware of it. One shoulder bumped his, offering support.

"*Ja.*" He drew a breath that was more like a gasp. "I'm okay."

"That was some show in the quilt auction," Zach said easily. "It's getting quite the reputation for excitement. Pretty soon people will come just for the drama, not for our school."

In spite of Alden's emotional turmoil, the corners of his lips twitched. "Were you there?"

"Yep. The whole family got to see my sister's quilt set a record." From his tone, he wasn't sure this was such a *gut* thing.

"You saw who won the bidding."

"I did. I wish it had been you. At least you'd have a use for it. I can't imagine a movie star knowing what to do with a quilt. He'll probably hang it on the wall."

"I hope he has a wall, then." He found himself strolling next to Zach without quite knowing how he'd got moving.

"I spent all yesterday with him, riding fence. He's got walls, all right. A bunch of them in a two-million-dollar house. Someplace called Seal Beach. Pretending to be someone else pays pretty well, I guess."

"Good for him," Alden said morosely.

Zach eyed him. "I'm not someone who pokes his nose into other people's business, but ... whoa. What possessed you?"

Alden sighed. If only Julie were here to explain her oh-so-smart makeover theory. "I'm never going to hear the end of this, am I?"

"Well, if Little Joe had announced your wedding date in church last week, I could kind of see it. But every Amish person in that tent knows you, and half of them had trouble keeping their eyes in their heads every time your hand went up."

Alden raised his face to heaven, but the blue skies merely smiled down on him. "I saw my mother and sisters' faces. And even that didn't stop me. You said it right, Zach. I must have been possessed."

"Auction fever," his friend said comfortingly. "It happens."

"I always thought of myself as a rational guy. Prudent, even. Cautious with my money, always trying to get the best deal for my dollar. But in there? All that went out the window. All I could think of was keeping her quilt out of his hands. No matter what it took."

"It's a nice quilt," Zach agreed. "Or is there more to it than that?"

Alden realized that he should have reined in his mouth about five minutes ago.

"I think you showed pretty much everyone in the district that you have feelings for my sister," Zach said. "It was news to me. Was it to Malena?"

"Probably." He prodded an antique plow blade with the toe of his boot. "She doesn't know I'm alive."

Zach chuckled. "She does now. Every girl in the district does. And by tonight, every girl in St Ignatius and beyond will, too."

None of the others mattered. But he couldn't very well say that to Malena's brother. "How am I going to look her in the face? Maybe I'd better skip the singing tomorrow."

"That'll leave a seat free for Cord, I guess."

Shock tingled down Alden's neck. "What?"

"Apparently he's interested in going. Something about singing glees and the nineteen forties. I don't know. Doesn't make much sense to me, but then, nobody is asking what I think."

Alden's despondency abruptly kindled into something hotter. "Cord McLean no more belongs at Bontragers' tomorrow night than I do in a movie theater."

Zach shrugged. "Nothing in the *Ordnung* says that an *Englischer* can't come to singing. In some places back east, they're even welcome in church, and the preacher gives the sermon in *Englisch*."

But Alden didn't care about other places. He cared about the Siksika, and Cord McLean weaseling his way in where he didn't belong.

"I can't take it," he muttered. "I'm going to hitch up and go."

"Do Rose and the girls have a ride home?"

"They brought the family buggy. I've got the wagon for the things I bid on."

"All right. If I see one of them, I'll tell them."

He managed to nod before he made his escape across to the pasture, where Joseph was surprised to have his enjoyment of the grass interrupted. "Come on, *mei freind*," he told the animal as he led him over to the wagon. "I'm no company for anyone just now. But you've got broad shoulders, haven't you?"

Joseph nodded as Alden backed him in, then fastened the buckles, and ten minutes later they were on their way. At a much faster clip than the horse was accustomed to.

§

MALENA DIDN'T KNOW HOW SHE GOT THROUGH THE REST OF the auction. She moved like a puppet—pegging quilts up and then taking them down. Up, then down. She had no idea who bid on what, or what the amounts were. Not after the sale of lot six. She had never felt so *verhuddelt* in all her life—not even this past Christmas, when Joshua had found a baby in a basket on the back porch.

When the buyers began trickling in from the cashier's shed, she asked Julie Stolzfus, who looked as pale and wide-eyed as she probably did, to take over her job pegging up the quilts with Ruby. As the person in charge of the quilt auction, it was now time for her to check the buyer's receipt and hand over a quilt to its new owner.

Glacier Lily's buyer didn't show up after the woman who had won the bid for lot five took her quilt. Which was just as well, for the woman was so thrilled that she could hardly stop talking. Lot seven came and went, and by the time the bidding began on lot eleven, Earth and Stars—she was seriously begin-ning to wonder if Cord was coming for his quilt at all.

He had to come. They couldn't very well accept his two thousand dollars and not give him the quilt.

Her quilt. Her beautiful Glacier Lily, that she had so hoped—

No, she couldn't let that thought roost in her mind.

Alden had been forced to stop bidding and thank goodness for that. She was *glad* he'd dropped out. It was an outrageous amount of money, and only someone like Cord McLean would spend it in such a reckless way, good cause or not. She had been astounded that Alden had wanted the quilt enough to spend two hundred dollars, for pity's sake.

But as the bidding had climbed, she'd become more and more frantic. She'd wanted to shout, "Stop! You can't afford to bid against him!"

But of course she hadn't. It wasn't her place. She wasn't his wife, or even his special friend.

As it was, the whole debacle would be talked of for months. He would never hear the end of it, and worse, every eye would be on her, looking for signs of *Schtaat*. Pride. The quilter whose work had set a record at the school auction.

Is she getting a swelled head? people would ask among themselves.

More important, will she raise the prices of her quilts? That'll show she thinks she's somebody now.

Malena nearly groaned aloud. Hadn't Rose predicted that very thing the other day in the quilt shop? Maybe she'd better have a word with her about knocking a hundred dollars off the price of the one in the window. Maybe—

"Are you going to give that to me, or make me work even harder for it?"

She came out of her panicked reverie to find herself once again holding the Glacier Lily protectively against her chest, like a baby, with no memory of having picked it up. She raised her gaze to see Cord McLean standing there, hipshot, a cocky grin on his face. Behind him was the man with the big camera on his shoulder.

In one movement, she brought the quilt up high enough to hide everything but her eyes.

It was now protecting her.

"Ease up, Kyle, my friend," Cord said over his shoulder. "Shoot her from behind while we do this, okay?"

"I don't want to be in your film," she got out, her breath beating on the thin plastic around the quilt.

"No one will know it's you," he assured her. "There are half a dozen girls wearing dresses and bonnets just like yours."

The seafoam green had been popular among her and Rebecca's buddy bunch, all right. But none of them had intractably curly red hair that always managed to escape their *Kapp*. And it wasn't a bonnet. Bonnets were black, and worn when you went to town. But she had no voice to correct him.

He made a show of taking the quilt from her, smiling over her shoulder at the camera. "Glacier Lily will look amazing in my house," he told it in what must be his actor's voice. "It will always remind me of Lincoln County, the Siksika Valley, and of a pretty Amish quilter whose name I can't say."

Let me out of here.

But she couldn't leave. She had work to do. "Cord, a line is forming behind you. Please let these ladies collect their quilts."

Thank goodness he was still acting. Like a gentleman, he laid the quilt over one arm and walked away with it, the camera following every move.

"That was Cord McLean." The woman in the green windbreaker, who had won the bid on Earth and Stars, was goggle-eyed. "Was that your quilt he outbid me on?"

"Yes." Malena checked the receipt and handed over the quilt, managing to remember to smile.

"You're so lucky," the teenager with the woman said on a sigh. "Now you're connected to him through your art."

"I don't think an Amish girl is allowed to be any such thing, honey," the woman said.

Malena only gave a weak tremble of the lips that she hoped looked like a smile, and the pair walked off. At least the woman looked happy with the quilt she'd won the bid on.

The auction ended at noon, but it took until nearly one to check everyone's receipts and clear the shelves in the back of the purchased quilts. Four still remained, looking lonely without their fellows.

"It happens every year," Ruby said. "People don't want to carry things around, I guess, and leave them here until closing."

"But the flower sale is next," Malena said. "They could get lost in all the coming and going."

"I know." Ruby shrugged. "But we can't very well stay here and guard them. Let's leave them with Mamm. That way, when they go to pay, it will save them a trip back here. I'm starving. Want to get some lunch?"

"*Ja.* We'll each take two."

Sadie promised to keep the quilts safe, and their little group headed for the schoolhouse, where the food vendors, both Amish and *Englisch*, were selling not only neatly wrapped baked goods, fruit, and vegetables, but there was a counter for hot food, too. Remembering what Susan had said, Malena sampled the Zook brothers' new goat cheese. Definitely delicious. But what was really satisfying was a Reuben sandwich from the hot food counter, melting with cheese and stuffed with so much pastrami and sauerkraut she could hardly get her mouth around it.

The sandwich hadn't been named after Dat, of course. But she enjoyed it partly because of its name.

At the sink outside, she found herself washing her hands next to Julie Stolzfus. Who looked troubled.

"I want to talk with you about something," she said hesitantly. "Do you mind if we don't go back in right away?"

"Not at all." It felt *gut* to stand in the shade of the oak tree that had sheltered the schoolhouse for years before she'd even been born. Mothers with small, exhausted children sat in the grass under it, enjoying the shade and people watching, greeting friends, and talking among themselves. Sara Fischer was one of them, and there was Mamm, laughing as baby Deborah tasted a spoonful of ice cream and withdrew in horror at the cold.

The Yoders' ice cream freezing contraption, which ran on a gas-powered engine, stood under a canopy right next to them, chugging away while David Yoder and his mother did a brisk business. Malena tried not to appear as though she was looking over the line of customers for Alden.

"Are you waiting for someone?" Julie asked.

Malena blushed. "*Neh.* Someone said they'd buy me an ice cream cone, but we didn't really set a time. I heard it was strawberry cheesecake."

"*Ja*, it is." Julie nibbled on the inside of her cheek, then seemed to make up her mind. "Please don't think I'm butting in. I'm not, truly. But I thought you'd want to know that my brother has gone home."

Another girl might have asked, *Why would you think that?*

Another girl might have said, *Who is your brother, again?*

But Malena had never been very good at prevaricating. Not with words. And certainly not in her face, which Mamm had often said was more than a window to her soul—it was an open door, letting everybody see exactly what was inside.

All she said was, "Oh." But Julie could still read her face.

"I'm sorry. I'm sure he is, too. I know he really wanted to buy you that ice cream. But after this morning—"

When she didn't go on, Malena said, "The auction?"

Julie took a breath, then blew it out. "This is me talking. I don't know what he really thinks. But he made a spectacle of himself. I think he's afraid to face you."

"Why should he be afraid? We're friends."

"Yes. That's the problem."

Malena was beginning to wonder if she was going to have to shake whatever Julie wanted to say out of her, the way she shook Grossmammi's stubborn Pippin to make an apple fall. "There's a problem?"

"I tried to tell him. An ice cream is one thing. But nearly two thousand dollars is a whole other thing."

Malena gave up. "Just spit it out, Julie. I don't understand what you're getting at."

"I told him, start small. With an ice cream cone. Something she likes. Then go from there. I never meant he should go crazy and do—that." She waved at the auction tent, where the flower sale was getting under way.

"Are you telling me … you gave Alden advice on …" She hardly knew how to finish. Color was already tingling into her cheeks and down her neck.

"On beginning a courtship. Letting you know he likes you. Once he'd bought you the ice cream, then I was to ask you if you'd like a ride home with him after singing tomorrow."

Only he'd gone home. Before any of that could happen.

Maybe he didn't want to face her after making a spectacle of himself, like Julie said. Or maybe the whole thing had shown him that liking her would only get him into trouble. That she wasn't worth what it was going to do to his reputation, even now. Who knew—maybe liking her would result in his losing business. Because once again, she was too much. Too notice-able. Not humble and self-effacing like an Amish woman was supposed to be.

"What do you think, Malena? Is that still possible? A ride home?"

With God all things are possible. But in this situation, it seemed, she was going to have to take that on faith.

"I don't think so, Julie," she said at last. "Cord McLean wants to come with us. So we'll have to babysit him. And make sure he doesn't bring his camera crew with him."

And after that, she didn't have the heart to rejoin the other girls at the picnic table. So she simply walked away and in a minute, lost sight of Julie's woebegone face in the crowd.

ALDEN HAD USED A ROPE AND PULLEY ASSEMBLY HE'D BUILT to lift the iron stock and the drill press out of the wagon, and then made Joseph comfortable in his stall at the back of the shop until it was time for them both to go home. It wasn't even three o'clock. So he'd opened up the shop, put the rack of wrought-iron kitchen implements outside the door to attract walk-ins, and busied himself getting organized for the jobs he had lined up the following week.

He tried to imagine how he would feel if he now owned Malena's quilt but couldn't pay the rent. But that was a dead-end road, wasn't it? He didn't own it, and the money would be in the bank on the thirty-first. He couldn't say he was happy about either fact, though.

Maybe the unhappiness could be laid at Cord McLean's door. Was it really true that he was coming to singing? But Zach had said so, and if anyone would know, it would be him.

Alden sighed and laid out the three work orders, one of which was shoeing the second string of the Rocking Diamond trail horses with Doc MacDonald. It would take a couple of days. The pay was *gut*, and if he could just avoid the movie star, he would be satisfied.

Someone stepped into the doorway and cast a shadow into the shop. Someone in a dress.

He looked up with a businesslike smile, expecting an *Englisch* tourist, and blinked the sun dazzle out of his eyes. His stomach did a backflip.

"Alden?" Malena said. "Are you open?"

"*Ja*. Figured I might as well be, since I was here."

"Why did you leave so early?"

"Why did you?" And how did she get here?

"I asked first." She stepped inside, still in the sunbeam, which made the curls escaping her *Kapp* look like they were on fire.

"I was disappointed about losing the bidding," he blurted. Even if he'd wanted to try to save face, she could probably see the truth written all over him. Besides, saving face was a prideful habit.

"I'm glad you lost," she said fiercely, taking two steps toward him as he stood at the order desk. "If you'd been unable to pay your bills because of me, I'd have been so upset, you can't even imagine."

"It wouldn't have been because of you," he said. "The money goes to the school."

"But it was my quilt. Honestly, Alden, I'll make you one if you want it. You don't have to bankrupt yourself."

She made it sound so easy. As though creating beauty like that didn't matter very much. When all those hours of work made it matter deeply. At least, to him. Funny to think that maybe to her, it really was just a quilt.

He had to change the subject, and right now.

"How did you get to town?" He moved away from the desk, from her, and wandered over to the smithing furnace, which of course was cold.

"Cord gave me a ride."

That was the last thing he'd been expecting. When his mouth opened but nothing came out, she smiled.

"I know. I was walking through the parking lot heading for the road, and he was putting Glacier Lily in the cab of his truck. Thank goodness the camera people were already pulling out."

"Maybe he figured that if there was no camera, there was no point in staying."

"Maybe. It wouldn't surprise me. But he asked if I was leaving and could he give me a ride home. I said I was going into town, so he dropped me off at the variety store."

And what had happened in those five miles that she wasn't mentioning? He'd seen them together. He gazed down at the work orders without seeing them. "Do you need something?"

"I need to talk to you. But on the way..."

Something in her tone made his stomach twist like a wrung-out dishcloth. "What happened?"

A flush burned into her cheeks. "He kept his hands to himself, if that's what you mean. But he asked me out. Can you imagine?"

He sure could. The sheer nerve, the complete wrongness of it made the air back up in Alden's lungs.

"He said he still had the private cabin booked because his trainer isn't here. He asked if I wanted to come over and watch one of his movies tonight. The carriage-racing one. He'd have the cook bring us dinner and we could eat on ... our laps, I guess."

He thought of the Miller dinner table, of their own at home, full of conversation and laughter and sometimes argument, but always love. Who asked a girl out just to watch TV and not talk? You asked her out on a date to get to know her, not to show off the fact you were in a movie.

Mind you, the last thing Alden wanted was for Cord McLean to get to know Malena at all. She was Amish. A church member. Surely she wasn't considering it. "What did you say?"

"I said no, of course. What do you think? I told him Dat would never allow it. And then he said that he'd come over and talk to him, reassure him that everything would be above board."

Alden could just imagine Reuben's reaction to *that*.

"So is he going to?"

"He would have, so I had to think of something else, really fast. He's used to getting what he wants. I had to find a way to make him stop this foolishness once and for all, or he'd never quit asking. Just like in cowboy training. The man never stops until he gets his own way."

"So ... what did you do?"

The flush deepened in her face.

He waited, unsure whether he wanted to hear the answer. *I said yes after all.*

She took a deep breath. "I said I couldn't, tonight or any night, because I had a boyfriend."

He stared at her. "You do? I've never heard a word."

"That's because he doesn't exist. Yet. So I came here to ask you, and hope to goodness you won't make a liar out of me."

Her words echoed in his head, but he couldn't make them make sense.

"None of our friends have to know. You know how the *Youngie* are. Private. We don't go flaunting our special friends in singing or making a big show of holding hands in public. Well, except for Susan. And she doesn't seem to care about anyone's opinion but Simeon's."

Alden didn't care two hoots about Susan's pursuit of Simeon King. He was still trying to recover from the fact that Malena Miller was asking him to be her special friend, not because she liked him, but because she needed a way to fend off Cord McLean.

"Please?" Those eyes the color of alpine gentians gazed up at him, pleading. "Just for two weeks. Just until he's gone. And then we can go back to normal."

Normal was never going to be normal again.

"What ... would I have to do?"

Her shoulders relaxed and the strained look around her eyes began to smooth out. "Well, I haven't really thought it through. Drive me home from singing, I guess, to start with? Julie said you wanted to ask."

So his sister had done her part, even after he'd fled the school grounds. He had better make her something nice this week, as a thank-you.

"That's what gave me the idea," she went on. "I thought maybe you were the one person who wouldn't laugh and tell me I was going overboard."

"I don't think you are," he said. "What about your family, though?"

"I'll just say as little as possible. Maybe you might come in Sunday night, for a snack. After all, you stayed for *Kaffee* the other day. Mamm wouldn't be very surprised."

She might if she knew what her daughter was up to. But Alden's mind was moving now, like the wind across the grassy meadows. Two weeks. He had two weeks of being Malena's fake boyfriend. Of being as close to her as he could ever dream, but had never really believed could happen.

In two weeks, could he show her his heart? Would she discover that, like him, she wanted a real relationship, not a fake one? That she could run toward him, not simply away from somebody else?

Alden made up his mind.

"All right," he said, with a smile. "Special friends it is, for two weeks. Let's think about ways we can show him we're a couple. On Sunday we'll make some plans, *nix*?"

Malena's relief and delight were a glow that warmed his spirits like a fire on a winter morning. "I could just hug you."

A sound assaulted his ears—one he'd heard before. "Now's your time. I can hear his truck coming. Let's stand in the doorway and give him something to think about."

And just as the big Ford went past, Malena flung herself into his arms.

For the first time, Alden held her, warm and vibrant and full of life. It almost made up for the fact that it was all an act.

For now.

9

MALENA HAD HALF EXPECTED—HOPED—THAT, Sunday being his day off, Cord McLean would be caught up in whatever was going on at the Rocking Diamond and forget that they would be going to singing. So her Sunday was a welcome day of calm and peace after the bustle and busyness of the auction. It had closed at five, and by seven Saturday evening, the men of the community had taken down the tents, put away the benches, and loaded up anything that hadn't sold in a rented truck to go back to the artisans who had made it.

Fortunately for her peace of mind, the four remaining quilts had been picked up by their new owners. And Sadie Wengerd had confided that, even though they had changed the date to be the end of summer instead of the beginning, they had brought in a respectable amount for the school—so much that she was sure it could be a permanent change.

"I don't know about that," Rebecca said Sunday afternoon, as they were writing letters. "August is a pretty busy month, what with canning and pickles and roundup right around the corner."

Malena had to agree. "How many of those folks came for the auction, and how many because they heard Cord McLean might be there?"

But luckily, decisions like that were up to the bishop's wife, not to her. Right now, all she had to do was finish this letter to Adam and Kate, and then maybe go for a ramble in the hills.

With Alden.

The thought flashed into her mind so suddenly she stopped writing. If she'd been *Englisch*, she could have pulled her phone out of her pocket and called him. But she didn't have one, and of course he wouldn't be at the shop to answer his on a Sunday.

It turned out she couldn't go for a walk anyway, because they heard the crunching of wheels in the gravel. Here came the King buggies rolling up the lane, and Susan Bontrager materialized out of thin air, though she was supposed to be helping her mother get ready for singing, and before you knew it, everyone was staying for supper. Which was all very well for Rebecca and Noah, and Susan and Simeon, and Joshua and Sara, and even Daniel and Lovina, who came over with Noah for supper every Sunday. Malena and Zach were like a pair of lone geese who had lost their mates—or simply not found them yet.

Never mind, she consoled herself. *You're getting a ride home with Alden later. You won't be alone then.*

She was hardly ever alone. She liked being with people, liked a bustle. But these days, even in a crowd, even among her family, she felt ... lonely. Missing what Rebecca had, what three of her brothers had. She wanted to have someone to confide her deepest feelings to. Someone who would be there no matter what, the way Daniel was for Lovina, and she was for him. Someone whom *Kinner* could look up to as an example of a godly man, who put church and family before himself, and was happy in doing it.

Was Alden like that?

She didn't know. Until that moment at the table the other day, when she'd caught his eye and couldn't resist laughing, he'd just been there in the background. One of the *Youngie*. Nice. Quiet, and not given to horseplay or pranks, like Cal and Dave Yoder. He helped his mother provide a home for his sisters. He was friends with Zach, which wasn't surprising, since Zach was the quiet type, too.

Alden Stolzfus was probably the most unlikely young man in the whole valley to play fake boyfriend. Cal Yoder would have eaten it up, and then some. But somehow she felt as though she could put her confidence in Alden and he wouldn't mishandle it. He didn't mind being used as a protective shield. And in doing that—she felt a squeeze of guilt as she realized it—she was causing him to be a little bit deceitful to the *Gmee*.

It wasn't forever. Only for two weeks, until Cord McLean left town. People dated for that long and then decided it wasn't right. They could do the same. Look at Rebecca—she had survived pretending to be engaged. That had been pretty awful, but … Malena and Alden weren't engaged. Not even close.

On second thought, it wasn't the same at all.

Arlon and Kate King had gone home, leaving Simeon to take his sisters and Susan over to Bontragers'. She and Zach, Noah and Rebecca would go together in Noah's buggy if Cord didn't show up. Malena had just dared to think that he wouldn't, when she heard a jaunty whistle in the lane. In a moment, there he was, dressed just as she'd last seen him, in a pair of Wranglers and a plaid shirt with mother-of-pearl snap buttons.

Both real cowboys and fake ones wore outfits just like this. But the Amish cowboys were plainly dressed in their Sunday clothes—black pants and waistcoats, and white shirts. Cord looked like a parrot next to a couple of magpies.

Malena sidled up to her twin. "Can we fit five in Noah's buggy?"

Rebecca eyed her. "You know we can."

"Can I sit with you two?"

With a flick of her lashes, Rebecca understood the situation. "Better with us than a worldly man."

But of course the worldly man had to make a fuss about it.

"Aw, Malena, I don't bite. You don't have to squash yourself in up there."

Noah shook the reins over his horse's back and they rolled out. Rebecca sat next to him, with Malena on the end by the passenger door.

"I'd be more squashed back there with you and my brother," she retorted. "At least Rebecca is slender."

"Hey," he said, pretending to be offended. "I'm keeping my weight down. What you see here is all muscle."

She didn't want to see anything, thank you very much.

With no reaction from her, he turned his attention to Noah. "I can drive a buggy. Any chance you'd let me take the reins?"

"Nope," Noah said easily. "My horse doesn't know you. I don't want him giving you trouble out here on the highway. Too dangerous."

"It's only a mile."

"That it is."

Noah was the nicest, kindest person in the world. But once he made up his mind, he was immovable. Cord was like a mosquito beating on a screen door. It did the door no harm at all, but the mosquito just got bent out of shape and frustrated.

Zach took Cord in hand when they got to Bontragers', where everyone was standing around in the yard catching up until Susan, their hostess, was ready to begin. He introduced him to those who hadn't met him yesterday, and, bless him, kept him at his side as they filed in to the living room. Tables had been set up, the green hymnbook and the *Christian Hymnal* laid at each place. Girls on one side faced boys on the other. Malena made sure that, while her twin and Noah sat facing each other, she was on Rebecca's other side, far from Cord.

Instead, she found herself facing Alden.

And there was that smile again, with the long dimple in his cheek that only seemed to appear when happiness mixed with just a touch of mischief. She was beginning to really like that smile. Good things happened around a smile like that, and after being enclosed in a buggy with Cord McLean, she could use some good.

As hostess, Susan chose the first song, courteously making it one that Cord might know—"Take Me Home, Country Roads." And then to balance it, one of the boys picked "Wings of a Dove." Cord didn't know that one, so Noah shared his songbook with him.

When they included one of the slow songs, in *hoch Deitsch*, of course, Cord didn't sing. For one, there were no musical notes in the *Ausbund* because everyone knew the melodies. And for two, the old Germanic printing was difficult to read if you weren't used to it. But at least he listened respectfully.

And then Malena stopped paying attention to Cord, because for the first time, she was sitting close enough to Alden to hear him sing. It wasn't the Amish way to stand out in any crowd, including a Sunday night singing. And he didn't. But all the same, sitting right across the table from him, she could appreciate the warmth of his voice and the sincerity in it. He sang, "There is rest, there is peace in the fold," and it was clear he really believed it.

Somehow, that was a comfort. Even with her silly plan to fend off Cord McLean, with Alden in it with her, she felt peace.

The *Youngie* usually sang for about an hour. They would break for a snack, and then sit down again to sing half an hour longer. Even before the break, Malena could tell that Cord was getting restless. Whatever idea he'd had in his head about glees in the forties was clearly not being performed here. Worse, theirs was not a group that sang parts, as they did in some communities, in keeping with the church's belief in an individual not standing out. She might feel bad for him if it hadn't been for the knowledge that next week, he'd be back at the Rocking Diamond. Then she'd be safe and could sing as freely as she would on any other Sunday.

After the last song had been sung, Malena and Simeon's two sisters helped Susan clean up the kitchen as the *Youngie* went out into the yard in twos and threes. Noah and Rebecca, as a couple publicly acknowledged, attracted less ribbing and teasing as he helped her into the buggy than, say, she and Alden would. But she could still hear the jokes through the open kitchen window. Beth and Julie had come with Alden, and were going home with the Yoder girls, who lived in town not far from the little house their family rented to Rose Stolzfus.

That left Alden to catch her eye as he passed through the kitchen from the bathroom down the hall. He was going to hitch up his horse. In spite of herself—in spite of the knowledge that this was pretend—Malena's heart picked up its pace.

She dried the last of the cake plates as fast as she could, while Susan stacked them in the cupboard. Barbara and Patricia King discreetly went outside to wait for Simeon, and Malena seized her chance to do the same when he walked into the kitchen to say good night to Susan. She slipped out through the kitchen door and on to the wide plank porch, where in the evenings the family could sit outside and enjoy the moon rising over the mountains.

Now, all she had to do was make her way down the drive to the road, escaping Cord's notice, and Alden would pick her up with no one the wiser.

"Malena? Is that you?"

Cord McLean stepped out of the shadows and she felt as though she had walked into a glass window.

"*Ja*, it's me. What are you doing out here?"

He stuffed his hands in his pockets. "I'm not sure where my ride is, or what I'm supposed to be doing."

"Aren't you going home with Zach?"

"Well, that's the thing. Rebecca took off with that guy who brought us. I can't find Zach at all. At least I knew where you were. This isn't very well organized, is it?"

Who was he to criticize? "We do this every week. It doesn't really need to be organized."

"So are we going now?"

"Zach will be along in a minute. I have a ride home."

He waited for a beat of silence, as though he thought she might explain. "Oh," he said on a note of discovery. "The boyfriend. I forgot."

Of course he had. If something didn't touch him, go on a

fork and into his mouth, or offer itself for him to sit on, it may as well not exist.

"Keep your voice down, all right?"

"Why?" he whispered. "Is it a secret? Something you don't want your parents to know?"

"Of course not. It's just our way. If a man is courting some-one, he's teased about her something awful. Most men don't like that, so they just pick the woman up as they're leaving."

"So who's picking you up?"

"It's not polite to ask, Cord."

"I don't care about being polite. I feel responsible for you. I want to see that you get home safely."

In a pig's eye, as their *mammi* used to say with a snort when she was alive. "Home is a mile away. On a beautiful night like tonight, with a half moon to see by, I could walk and get home safely. And have done, many a time."

She could hear a horse in the yard, and the jingle of harness.

"I have to go."

"But—"

"Zach is probably in the barn hitching up. Don't panic—no one is going to leave you to walk home all alone."

"That's not why—"

But Malena had run out of time for chatter. "See you at breakfast."

She ran down the porch steps and hurried up the lane. Unlike the Circle M, the Bontrager ranch was situated on open land. There weren't trees growing in clusters where a person could wait discreetly until the buggy drew up beside her. On the good side, many of their buggies looked the same, so it was hard to tell who was driving whom. The ones that were different, such as the Holmes County ones with the angled bottom, or the yellow ones from Indiana, usually didn't belong to the young men, but to their parents. When they reached courting age, boys ordered what they wanted from the buggy maker in the style determined by the *Ordnung*, and it came on the train. As their parents' buggies from away aged and became unreliable, the new ones were made in the Montana style. Within another generation, the Mountain Home buggies would all look the same, and no one would stand out unless they were brand new to the community.

Alden's buggy rolled to a stop beside her and she climbed in without hesitation.

She sniffed. "It smells new still. You got it, what, three years ago?"

"*Ja*. As soon as I could afford it. And I sure do take good care of it." He paused. "I saw Cord McLean waiting around outside. Did you see him?"

"Mm-hm. He wanted to know when we were going home. He thinks the singings are disorganized."

Alden chuckled. "Sorry to hear that. I suppose roundup looks disorganized, too, to someone from away who doesn't know how it works."

"Little do they know it runs like a finely oiled clock. Well, most of the time. We had a little excitement last year when Joel got lost on the mountain, but it turned out all right."

"Daniel would never let anything happen to him."

"I know it. And he didn't. Joel thought it was all a grand adventure, but I bet Lovina got her first gray hair over it."

In the light of the battery-powered buggy lamps, she could see he was still smiling. "I have to say, I'm glad things will be back to normal before roundup."

"Me, too." Neither or them had to define what *normal* meant: Cord McLean gone from the valley, back to his own life. "For the next two weeks, though, I suppose we'd better figure out what we're doing."

"Giving you a ride home," he said, as though counting on his fingers. "And next Sunday, remember, church and singing are at the Zook brothers' place."

"Technically, they are single, so they can sing with us." They both grinned. Willard and Hezekiah Zook were confirmed bachelors in their fifties, and every time the singing was there, the women had to arrange among themselves who was going to act as hostess and chaperone. It wasn't potluck— those two men were as handy in a kitchen as any woman, and Malena wasn't the only one who looked forward to doings there. But a married woman had to be nominally in charge for the single women's sake.

"So that's Sundays taken care of," Alden went on. "And volleyball is Friday night at Yoders'."

"I can ask Dat if we can have a fishing frolic, maybe on Cord's last day," she suggested. "That is, if he hasn't run screaming from the ranch by Wedesday."

"We can always hope." He was so deadpan she had to laugh.

"It would be a good opportunity to do two things at once— fish for our supper, and give him a nice sendoff."

Alden was slowing the horse to make the left turn into the Circle M lane. Were they home already?

"That was a pretty fast mile," he said.

Their thoughts seemed to be running in the same channels again. It was kind of refreshing. Usually Malena didn't experience that with anyone but her twin.

"Will you be all right at home with him?" Alden asked quietly, all levity drained away.

"He's out at work during the day, and he's so tired by nightfall that he goes to bed at almost the same time as Dat and Mamm. So I really only see him at meals, when the whole family is there. Honestly, I think he was just bored, yesterday and today."

"Or maybe you're familiar, and he needed to be around you."

Unlikely, she thought. "I guess he misses his staff. Or the people who are always wanting pictures. They're probably familiar, and around him all the time."

"I don't think it was that. There's something about you that draws people, like a fire on a cold day."

He pulled his horse to a stop near the steps to the house, and wrapped the reins around the brake lever. When he put a hand to the door, he realized she hadn't moved. She was still staring at him, trying to get past her astonishment.

"What?" he said, one corner of his mouth quirking up. "It's true."

"And you think *he* felt that?" Somehow it was important to her that it was Alden who felt this way, not Cord.

"I don't know about him. But I do."

Heat climbed in her cheeks—she hoped he couldn't see it in the dark. "That's the nicest thing anyone's ever said to me."

"Plenty of people probably thought it."

"But you thought to say it." Then she remembered. "It's a nice way to begin our pretend courtship. *Denki.*"

"It wasn't pretend."

Oh my. Flustered, she slid aside her door. "My parents will be looking out the window any second if I don't get out of this buggy. Are you coming in for a snack?"

He took a deep breath and let it out. "Is Cord going to join you?"

"I expect so. We did kind of agree that you'd come in."

"I'll just tie up Timothy and be right there."

Malena let herself into the house to find Rebecca and Noah cuddled up on the sofa with mugs of what smelled like hot chocolate. "Alden is right behind me."

"And somebody's behind him," Noah said, as they all heard another buggy coming down the lane.

"Zach, probably," Rebecca murmured. "Better put more *Millich* in the saucepan, *Schweschder*."

As she was filling it, she heard Alden come in, and the welcoming voice of her twin. Then he ambled into the kitchen to join her. Funny—he never seemed to move impatiently, but he had a long stride that got him where he was going sooner than she always expected.

"I hate to horn in on their time together," he said.

"They knew we were coming back afterward. Though I don't seem to remember a line-up for the sofa when Daniel was courting Lovina. Or Adam and Kate, for that matter. How did they all manage it?"

"Careful planning, I guess." He was about to say something more, when new voices came from the other room. And suddenly the kitchen and living room seemed to be filled with people. They were only six, but still—Cord McLean tended to fill up any space you put him in.

"Here's where the lovebirds are hiding," Cord said, taking in herself and Alden at a glance.

"Not hiding," Alden said. "Heating more milk for chocolate."

"That's your story," Cord said, nodding. "You tell it any way you like."

Since she was actually standing over the flame stirring the milk, this seemed a bit much, but there was no point in correcting him. "Alden, maybe you can pull the orange cupcakes out of the cooling cupboard. They're in the plastic tub with the blue lid."

"I'll get them," Cord said. "I know where they are."

An authority already on their cooking habits. "Don't worry about plates. We can eat off paper napkins."

It wasn't so much that Cord had decided to play the role of host. It was more like he was making a point to Alden that he had more of a place here than Alden did. Which made no sense—Alden had been coming here for work and church and doings with the *Youngie* for as long as he'd lived in the valley.

Malena let it go. No point in making a fuss when there were only three more days.

When she and her helpers carried the hot chocolate, cupcakes, and a bag of chips and homemade salsa out to the living room, Malena was surprised to see Ruby Wengerd among them.

"Hallo, Ruby. I thought these characters would have taken you home."

"I hope it's okay that I came along?" The young woman looked so worried that Malena regretted her thoughtlessness.

"Of course it's okay. Without you, we'd be outnumbered and these boys would eat all the cupcakes."

They settled around the food—except for Cord, who pointedly declined a cupcake. His loss, Malena thought as she bit into Rebecca's special recipe—orange cherry with orange flavored frosting. Sublime.

Alden reached over and touched the tip of her nose, as gently as a butterfly landing.

The shock of it tingled through her, right to her fingertips. She forgot where she was and who she was with. The room might have been empty, except for him.

10

MALENA'S HEART kicked into a gallop. She could hardly believe his daring at touching her in public. He looked as surprised at himself as she was. But someone had to do some-thing—say something—

He showed her his fingertip.

Frosting.

She let out a breath and chuckled. "*Denki.*" She must make it look like a joke. He was being playful, that was all. "Mamm says that when I was a baby, I enjoyed my food with my whole face. I guess nothing's changed."

"Deborah is like that now," Rebecca said, her easy tone smoothing the moment over. "It runs in the family."

"Nothing wrong with enjoying your food," Alden said. "God provided it for us—I'm sure He knows it shows gratitude."

"That's right," Ruby said, a smile in her quiet voice. "Imagine going to all the trouble of cooking a big meal, and people picking at it and complaining. I wouldn't want to make your mother feel that way, never mind the Lord."

"That's why we say grace, isn't it?" Noah said. "We say thank you before, and enjoying food is a way to say it during."

"Some churches say grace again afterward," Malena added.

"That's a lot of gratitude," Cord said, tipping his head back to toss a loaded corn chip into his mouth. "Especially for a bunch of people who just ate at ... what was their name?" he asked Zach.

"Bontragers'."

"You were the one who wanted to come," Malena reminded him. "Was it what you expected?"

He shook his head. "I didn't know what to expect. What's with the girls on one side, boys on the other?"

She lifted a shoulder. "It's the same in church."

"But you guys are dating."

Puzzled, Alden said, "So?"

"I don't know. You could hold hands under the table. That's a missed opportunity in my book."

"We don't display affection publicly like that," Noah told him. "If somebody did, they'd get ribbed about it forever."

"Besides, if we're singing a hymn, we're supposed to be thinking about the words and what they mean, not about who's holding our hand," Malena said.

"Is that what you do?" Cord's voice was a silky challenge. "Think about hymns and God and not about Stolzfus here?"

She was not going to let him tarnish those sweet moments of listening to Alden sing. Of being glad that of all the places she could be, she had managed to be right across from him through no planning of her own. As though *der Herr* had chivvied the two of them gently into place, right where He wanted them.

She lifted her chin. "What I think about in the privacy of my own mind is none of your business."

He laughed. "Gotcha. Of course you were thinking about your boyfriend. Nobody can be that religious."

The word seemed to echo in a room gone suddenly silent.

ALDEN COULD PRACTICALLY HEAR THE OTHERS WONDERING if they should reply or not. But someone had to say something. "I guess it depends on how you're brought up," he said in as measured a tone as he could muster. "Most people don't come into a person's home and criticize them, for instance."

Cord jumped on him like a rooster on a lizard. "I wasn't criticizing her."

"Glad to hear it."

Cord leaned back in the easy chair and a mask seemed to fall over his face. A mask that looked world-weary and a little dangerous. As though it might be one of the parts he'd played in the past, or was trying on for size. "You have something against me, Stolzfus?"

The room was still so quiet Alden could hear Naomi's engagement clock ticking on the oak mantel.

Malena shook her head, as though answering a different question. "No, that's not it. He's a working rancher, remember, not one of those men riding motorcycles. "He'd say *you got*, too. And more quietly, like he doesn't really care, because he's stared down a coyote and a mountain lion, and another man doesn't hold much of a threat for him."

What nonsense was this? Who was she talking about?

Cord stared at her, too, his eyes rounding slightly. "Are you giving me *notes*?"

"I don't know what that is, but whoever that was just now,

it wasn't you. And it wasn't this man you're going to play in *Ride Forever*."

Alden let out a long breath. Now he saw what she'd done.

"Well, I'll be." Cord rose and stood there a moment, hands on hips, shaking his head.

"There," she said, pointing at him. "My father does it just that way."

"You think I should play him like Reuben?"

Zach laughed, and Malena joined in. "If you did, it'd be an awfully quiet movie," Zach said. "Our father doesn't say much."

"But you have a point. I should be studying the characters I have all around me. They're authentic." He waved a hand vaguely in the direction of the downstairs bedrooms. "I have to make some notes. Good night."

And before anyone could say a word, he strode down the hall without even lighting a lantern. Alden hoped there was one in his room.

"What just happened?" Ruby wondered aloud in *Deitsch* when they heard the bedroom door close. "Did I miss a whole conversation somewhere?"

"Noah can tell you," Rebecca said, "if you'd like a ride home. It's pretty late to be out on the highway, and it's on his way."

"That'd be nice. *Denki*, Noah. Becca, I'd love the recipe for those cupcakes sometime. You know Dat's sweet tooth."

And just like that, the living room emptied. Ruby left with Noah, with whom it was safe to accept a ride because he was taken, and Zach and Rebecca went upstairs, leaving Alden alone with Malena ... just as if they really were courting.

Suddenly he didn't know what to do with his hands—the hands that made his living, that held the reins. The hands that still felt the softness of Malena's skin as he'd swiped away that bit of frosting. Better to put them to work.

He collected the dishes and took them into the kitchen, where Malena was already filling the sink with hot water.

"How did you manage to do that just now?" he asked quietly, aware that her parents' room was just on the other side of the wall.

She made a sound like *hmph*. "The quickest way to distract that boy is to make it about him. Did you see him pull on that face like a mask? I knew he was playing a part. So I pretended I was—oh, I don't know. A teacher?"

"You did well. And got rid of him, too. Bonus."

She huffed a silent laugh while he found a dish towel and began to dry their mugs. "I have to say I wasn't expecting our first date to be like this."

"This wasn't a date," he protested. "It was just a ride home."

"But it was interesting. Fun. Eventful." She turned her head to smile at him as she washed the saucepan, and he lost his train of thought.

Her skin looked as soft as a rose petal in the lamplight. And the twin dents in her cheeks just invited kisses pressed into each one. His gaze found hers. The saucepan made a muffled sound as it fell from loosened fingers and submerged itself in the soapsuds.

If she had been a magnet and he a piece of iron, he could not have resisted her pull any less. Her lips parted in surprise, as though something in her recognized something in him that she had never seen before.

He bent just a little—his lashes drifted down—

Someone cleared his throat and Malena sucked in a breath and seized the saucepan, scrubbing it within an inch of its life.

Reuben Miller's lips twitched as he opened a cupboard door. "Thought I might get a drink of water." He'd taken the time to pull on a pair of pants and a shirt before he came into the kitchen, though his feet were bare. "You still here, Alden?"

"Just—" Alden's throat closed. "Just helping Malena."

"I see that."

What did he mean? Alden's thoughts flapped around in his skull like crows scared out of a tree.

"Cord go out?" He drained the glass of water and handed it to his daughter.

"Neh." Malena washed it, handed it to Alden, then pulled the plug and scrubbed down the sink. "He went to his room just before the others left."

"He's here?" Malena nodded. "Well. *Gut.* Means he'll get up at the regular time." He walked over to the entry to the hall. "Guess I'll leave you two. Don't be up too late."

"Dat, wait." Malena hung the cloth up to dry and leaned on the counter as her father came back in. "Cord's last day is Wednesday. What if we had a fishing frolic and fish for supper?"

Reuben nodded. "Sounds good. You're sure he's leaving?"

"You agreed to a week, Dat. Unless his trainer comes. I'm going to run him through roping a hay bale from a moving horse tomorrow."

"I'm due at the Rocking Diamond to shoe their second trail string on Tuesday," Alden said.

Reuben moved a little closer, though they were speaking in *Deitsch* and even if Cord could hear, he wouldn't understand. "I have to say, I'll be glad when he moves on. Seems like all our conversations these days revolve around him. Not sure two hundred dollars a day is worth that. *Mei Fraa* says we may as well have a television in the house."

"I suppose an actor is the next best thing to having a movie walking around," Alden agreed with a grin.

"Sooner he's back where he belongs, the better I'll feel." Reuben's gaze settled on Malena. "You're all right, *Dochsder*? The burden seems to be falling on you and I'm regretting it."

"I'm all right, Dat. I've got Alden to protect me." She smiled up at him, and Alden felt the flush climbing in his cheeks. Somehow the thought of deceiving this man even a little felt wrong.

Malena clearly saw it. "I mean it, Dat. Alden and I are pretending to date so Cord will keep his distance."

That gaze, that could be so compassionate for a hurt calf or so full of laughter with delight in his children, chilled to the point Alden could almost feel the temperature drop. Like a storm front moving in on a sunny day.

"He giving you grief? If he is, he's off this property tonight."

Malena put a hand on her father's arm. "*Neh*, truly. He's done a bit of flirting, and the quilt auction—" When her throat closed, he put his own ropy hand over hers. "Well, I can't say I'm happy he won my quilt, but what's done is done," she finished softly. "Anyway, Alden agreed to pretend to be my boyfriend for two weeks. Until Cord is gone back to wherever he came from."

"Pretend, *nix*?" Reuben patted her hand and released it. "Does your mother know?"

"She will when you tell her." Malena's smile was full of relief that the truth was out. "This isn't like Rebecca's trouble in the spring. When everybody thought she was engaged—including Andrew King."

"If you say so." Reuben's gaze flicked to Alden. "What do you think about it?"

"I don't want him bothering her," he said as bluntly as Reuben ever could. "He's backing off already. But the rest of the family should know."

"Hm." Reuben turned back to Malena. "He's got no business looking at you, *Dochsder*. You're Amish. Baptized. What interest does he think you could have in a worldly man?"

"He doesn't know that, though, Dat. To him, it's just religion. Not a way of life. Not a commitment that can't be broken without ... eternal consequences."

"And you can't just explain that to him?"

"He'd mock it," Alden said. "Make light of it. He already has, when he tried to pick a fight this evening. Not that any of us are going to take him up on it, but it's clear this is the first time he's ever been around Amish folks. Better to hold him off using a way he understands."

"Only for two weeks," Malena stressed.

"I see." Reuben looked from one to the other, then turned for the door. "Shame it's about him again, *nix?*"

It took a good ten minutes before what he meant sank in, and by then, Malena was waving good-bye from the door.

As he untied his horse, Alden felt as though he'd just walked through an earthquake. Or more accurately, had a shakeup of the heart.

Reuben approved of Alden's courtship of his daughter.

Not for pretend. For real.

THE NEXT MORNING AT BREAKFAST, IT WAS ALL ALDEN could do to keep his mind on the things of this earth—such as conversation with his family that made sense, and actually eating what was on his plate. He forgot to take his thermal mug of coffee with him when he left, and had to turn around and walk back for it while Mamm waited for him at the end of the lane.

As he left the second time, Beth giggled behind the screen door and he distinctly heard the word *Freierei*. Courtship.

That hadn't taken very long. His sisters had eyes in their heads, and they'd probably seen Malena get into his buggy as they'd gone past. The funny part? As unlike him as this behavior was, he wasn't even pretending. He'd heard that love had several symptoms, like a tendency to stare off into space and forget things.

"Is everything well with you, *mei Soh*?" He and his mother walked to work each morning—it was only a couple of blocks and left the horse and buggy for the girls if they needed them.

"*Ja*, Mamm. I just didn't get much sleep last night, that's all."

"Thinking about Malena Miller?"

It was lucky he'd just swallowed a swig of coffee, or he'd have spat it down his shirt. "What?"

"A man doesn't bid nearly two thousand dollars on the quilt of just anyone."

"I've heard auction fever is real. Now I know."

"The first two hundred wasn't fever," his mother pointed out in the voice of experience. "I wish you had got Glacier Lily. But if not the quilt, then perhaps the *Maedsche* who made it?"

"Have you been talking to *mei Schweschdere*?"

"Who, me?" his mother said innocently. "Your sisters did mention that this actor is hanging around her a little too much. I'm surprised Reuben hasn't put a stop to it, since the man is right there in the house."

"Malena and I are putting a stop to it," he said, making up his mind not to dance around her question any longer. "We're pretending to court so that he backs off."

"Are you, now?" Her brows rose under her black away bonnet. "Do Reuben and Naomi know?"

"We told Reuben last night."

"I see. Know the difference between pretending and lying?"

"*Neh*, what?"

"There isn't one."

Trust Mamm to get right to the meat of the matter. "It's only for two weeks. Until Cord leaves the valley."

"And then what?"

"Then ... we pretend to break up. Or ..."

"Or you find out that courting a girl isn't just make-believe?"

"Something like that," he mumbled.

They parted at the intersection, where there was a gas station on one corner and a bar on the other, marking the official beginning of downtown. His mother walked across the highway and let herself into the quilt shop, where Malena's Amish Diamond quilt hung in the window. As he watched, Mamm gently removed the advertisement for the school auction from the glass, so as not to disturb the display of complementary fabrics she'd placed around the quilt.

Downtown was coming awake, with doors opening and racks of things to buy carried outside to be placed temptingly at the door. He'd best do the same, in case some of the folks who had driven a long way for the auction were still holidaying in the Siksika and the last of their money was burning a hole in their pockets.

His main task today was to start on a garden gate for the town's only bed and breakfast, a rambling farmhouse near the creek. A FOR SALE sign had been swinging in the wind in the front yard since spring, with no takers, apparently. The owners had done some sprucing up, including landscaping that included an herb and vegetable garden, discreetly fenced to keep the deer out. It was this fence that needed a nice wrought-iron gate.

Once he made the frame today, he'd leave the twisted bars and decorative curlicues for Thursday. If he was going to the Rocking Diamond tomorrow, he'd need to replace some inventory in the farrier wagon and make sure he had enough shoes and nails for the entire string of horses. He expected the job would be completed by Wednesday night, in time for the fishing frolic, but with horses, you never knew. Doc MacDonald might find injuries in the feet that would delay the process and mean another visit.

The morning went by quickly, and the afternoon, too. He even managed to sell two paper towel holders and an entire curtain rod set.

"I'm going to use this as a quilt rack," the *Englisch* woman said as he wrote up her receipt. "How perfect to have an Amish-made quilt rack. Now all I need is an Amish quilt. Were you at the auction on Saturday, young man?"

"I was," he said, handing the slip to her. He'd already put the turned rod, spiral finials, and wall brackets in her car. "I bid on the Glacier Lily, but didn't get it."

"I did, too!" She beamed at him. "Didn't take me long to drop out, though. Wasn't that something? I sure wish ... Never mind. I'll find one somewhere that doesn't cost two thousand dollars."

He indicated his mother's shop. "The same quilter made that one in the window."

The woman's eyes filled with surprise, then steely determination. She marched across the street to Rose Garden Quilts, and in a moment, the Amish Diamond came down from the rod it had been hanging on and was whisked into the interior of the shop.

A few minutes later, he watched the woman place the big plastic bag carefully in the back of the car, then drive away with the same kind of triumphant expression the hunters wore when they filled their tags. Good for her.

But he couldn't help a pang inside, even as he reminded himself Malena would appreciate her share of the price. Because there went another piece of her heart.

Ah well. On the bright side, it was kind of nice that her quilt would hang from his ironwork. Somewhere in Nevada, where the woman lived, a part of them would be together.

Even if no one else ever knew.

11

PRACTICALLY EVERY TIME Cord McLean's lasso fell over the horns tied to the hay bale, it seemed, he asked her out again. Finally Malena lost her patience.

"No, I don't want to go for ice cream. No, I don't need anything in town. And if you don't stop this nonsense, my father will ask you to leave."

"You could ask me to leave yourself." He grinned at her from the saddle, and Marigold patiently waited for him to stop talking and coil his rope. "But you won't. Because you like me."

"That is becoming less true every day."

"But it's still true."

Good grief. He never let up. She squinted up at him from under the brim of the raggedy barn hat she'd jammed over her *Duchly*. "Again, Cord. Circle to the right and throw with your near side arm."

She almost hoped he'd miss, which he did in two out of three tosses. The loop fell neatly over the horns, which meant he'd got two in a row.

"Good," she said. "Again. Make it three."

"How about if we—"

"Stop. Or I'll ask my parents to cancel the fishing frolic Wednesday night."

This was news to him, because she'd kept it quiet on purpose. "That's my last day here. You mean I get to frolic with you?"

Oh, if she could only slap Marigold's flank, make her jump, and unseat him! But that would not only be unwomanly, it would be mean to the poor horse, who was working harder than anybody in this corral.

"A frolic is what we call a work party."

"Oh." All the stuffing went out of him. "More work."

"Yes. It's what you're paying for, isn't it? To know how to handle the work? Anyway, fishing isn't work so much as having fun catching dinner. Some of the *Youngie*—I mean, the young folks from church—are coming over. Do you know how to use a fly rod?"

"Are you kidding? I saw *A River Runs Through It* when I was a kid. I learned during the summer. I have my rod and flies in the truck. I figured if there was anywhere to get them wet again, it would be Montana."

She did not ask what river was running through where. "This afternoon maybe you can go get a three-day license and brush up. Yoder's Variety Store carries them."

"Only if you go with me."

She glared at him. "Cord. Mountain Home is small. There's only one variety store. You dropped me there the other day. I'm sure you remember."

"It's more fun if you go with me."

"I'm quilting this afternoon, and I believe Zach has some work for you."

"You'd rather sew patches than go for a ride with me?" His

voice was plaintive, but the spark in his eyes told her he was teasing. Again.

"I'd rather sew patches than do anything." She reconsidered. "Except obey my parents and worship the Lord."

"Oh. Well. If you're going to bring the Lord into it, then I'm beaten before I start."

That was the great thing about *der Herr*. He was so much larger than anyone, yet His power was there for the asking to them that loved Him.

In the knowledge of that power, she said, "It's time for me to help with lunch. You can practice on your own if you like until Zach comes in, or take Marigold to the barn."

"Since you have better things to do than coach me like you promised, I'll practice."

She didn't dignify with a reply this pathetic attempt to get his way, simply escaped into the house. It was cool and welcoming after the heat and dust of the corral, and with relief, she pulled off her headscarf and straw hat. After washing her face and arms, she put on her *Kapp* and pinned it securely before she went out to the kitchen.

"He's improving," Sara said, slicing fat ripe tomatoes while baby Nathan entertained himself with a teething ring and made approving noises at the preparations for lunch.

"His roping is, anyway. Two in a row is progress. I just wish he'd talk less and concentrate more."

"I heard." Sara lifted her chin at the window, which was open to catch the breeze. "I don't know what he thinks he's going to gain. It's not that he's flirting with you. It's more like—"

"Boredom," Malena supplied, measuring flour and shortening for pie crust. "Where are the others?"

"Naomi and Rebecca and Deborah are out on the deck, taking in the washing."

It was Monday. Wash day in most of the Amish households in the valley.

"How many pies are we making?"

"Four. The venison and gravy are already done and waiting for you." Sara paused, and returned to the subject. "Maybe it is boredom. But it seems to me it's more like he has to win. Even if it's a contest only he's competing in. Because you sure aren't."

"Aren't what?" Rebecca came in the kitchen door, Deborah on one hip. "I made a big salad already. It's in the fridge. All we need is pickles and bread sliced. Competing in what?"

"That's the question," Malena said. "Who knows? Zach will earn his eternal reward if he gets Cord out of my hair this afternoon." She tried not to use the rolling pin as though the pastry was Cord's backside. "There's a design in my head I have to get down on paper and nothing is going to drag me away from it."

"Did you tell him about the fishing frolic?" Rebecca asked. "Does he fish?"

"Yes and yes. Though he hasn't for a long time. And can we not talk about him for five minutes? Dat said last night it was like having a television in the house."

Sara laughed. "I can vouch for the truth of that. All I can say is, thank goodness for Alden Stolzfus."

His name brushed across Malena's skin the way a breeze rippled across a calm lake. "His courting me is supposed to be pretend, but he really is nice. And easy to talk to."

"Which means mostly he just listens," Rebecca teased, cuddling Deborah at the table.

"Neh," she said a little defensively. "I don't talk *all* the time. But I'm glad he's my friend right now."

"Just a friend?" Sara eyed her. "Or might there be something more?"

Malena had no idea how to answer that. "I've only got to know him this past week."

"Well," Mamm said as she came through the screen door with a basket full of clean laundry, "with the spectacle he made of himself over your quilt, everyone in the valley knows he's sweet on you. Or was that pretend, too?"

Rebecca snorted. "If you ask me, eighteen hundred dollars is dead serious."

Mamm tilted her head in acknowledgement of this truth. "So maybe only one of you is pretending," she said slowly, watching Malena.

Malena was silent, crimping the edges of the pie crust automatically while her mind whirled. She hadn't wanted to think about what that crazy bidding contest at the auction really meant. But now it seemed so obvious, the truth as plain as Mamm's quiet voice. Did she dare think that Alden's actions were more than just auction fever? Or a competition between him and Cord that got carried away?

Had he wanted that quilt simply because she'd made it? Somehow, that moment at the sink Sunday night seemed to confirm it.

When the venison and potato and onion pies came out of the oven, she didn't dare come any closer to an answer. But even the possibility of Alden's going to such lengths for her sake made her feel warm in her heart. So different from the annoyance that Cord's words got roiling inside. One man gave her peace, the other agitation. If that wasn't the Lord making the way plain, she didn't know what was.

Of course, she thought as she climbed the stairs after lunch and found the haven of her combined bedroom and workroom once again, the Lord would never dream of pointing the way to a worldly man. But strangely, none of the Amish men in the valley gave her this sense of peace. Only Alden. Cal Yoder? Not for a minute. Even Dave was too rigid for comfort—which she only knew because of his very brief courtship of Rebecca. There were a few young men in the other church district on the far side of the valley—one of whom she'd dated last year—but again, this sense of peace had been missing when she'd been with him.

She got out her notebook and turned to a fresh spread of pages, seeking the happiness she always found there. Glacier Lily was lost to her forever, and she didn't have the heart to make another one. But there were other flowers native to their valley, weren't there? Lupines were a family favorite, with their blues and purples and delicate shades of lavender and pink. Malena's pencil sketched a grid and a spire of triangles formed. No, that wasn't it. The lupines themselves needed to be appliqué, like the glacier lilies had been. Lupines grew straight, and grew in communities. They sprang from a riot of leaves. Riot … movement … *pinwheels!* That was it. Lots and lots of pinwheels in shades of light and dark green, and maybe a touch of yellow.

When she came to herself two hours later, the rough sketch of Montana Lupine was laid out on the pages, clear enough to begin the arithmetic of triangle sizes and squares versus snowballs. It looked alive, with movement and joy as the lupine spires sprang up to create the central point that drew the eye.

It delighted her. And if a sketch in colored pencil could make her happy, then she was on the right track. The really special quilts, like Glacier Lily and Flying Home, had been gifts from *Der Herr*, who had shared just a tiny spark of His creativity with her. Not that she would ever say that aloud to anyone. But it had always seemed that way, ever since she was small, and she cherished His gift.

Another gift was hers this afternoon—the time to create. No Cord, no chores, no interruptions. Just herself and *Gott* and beauty, alone together with a job to do.

And when it was complete? She thought of Montana Lupine hanging up for sale in the window of Rose Garden Quilts, and felt a pang of dismay. No. It would be a gift, not sold. She didn't know who it was for, or what the occasion would be. The wedding quilt she was making for Joshua and Sara was already underway, and it was likely one for her twin and Noah would be right behind it. Rebecca liked lupines, but this didn't feel like Rebecca. Kate and Adam? No, Malena was already toying with a wreath for them, that combined the flowers of Pennsylvania with those of Montana. And a quilted border of pine trees and pine cones.

Ah well, there was no hurry to find a home for this newly born design.

It would come to her. It always did.

She was gazing into space, lost in the many ways she could calculate the piecing, when someone knocked on the bedroom door. It wouldn't be Rebecca or Sara, who would never interrupt if she was designing. But Mamm might need her.

"Come in."

The door swung open to reveal Cord McLean, who hesitated on the threshold.

Oh, for pity's sake. Was there no escaping this man? How had he got up here?

With one hand, she closed her notebook, and held up the

other as he took a step into the room.

"No," she said. "I'm very sorry, but this is my bedroom as well as my sewing room. It's not fitting for a man to be in here."

Taken aback, literally, the boot that had been raised to take a step inside settled on the threshold once more. "I just came to give you a message."

"It couldn't wait until dinnertime? I thought you were out with Zach."

"I was. We got done early. So I went to town and got a fishing license, like you said."

She gazed at him, wondering why on earth this was important enough to interrupt a person's work.

"Don't look so annoyed. I stopped in at the blacksmith shop and Alden said to tell you that the Amish Diamond sold today."

A twinge of regret that it was irrevocably gone competed with amazement that it had sold so fast. Amazement won. "Who to?"

"A lady from Nevada," he said. "How much do you get for a quilt when it's not at an auction?"

With a frown, she turned back to her notebook. "Whatever Rose Stolzfus thinks is fair. Which is between her and me."

"Oh, come on, Malena. I dropped two grand on your Glacier Lily, in front of the whole town. You've got no quilty secrets from me."

Trust him to rub it in. To embarrass her—make her feel obligated to him. And maybe she did feel a little obligated. It was a lot of money. But that didn't mean he could use that to manipulate her into sharing anything with him.

"I've got no secrets, quilty or otherwise. But my agreement

with Rose Stolzfus is business. Did Alden say anything else?"

"Yeah, he sends his undying love and wants to know when you're going to look at china patterns."

What on earth? Then she saw that light in his eyes, amusement with just a tiny trickle of malice. "He did not. Don't tell fibs."

With a grin, he said, "You know me too well."

"I can see the rocks at the bottom of a shallow stream, too."

Wincing—or pretending to—he said, "Direct hit. Who said Amish girls were meek and obedient?"

And now he was trying to make her feel bad about her example? "Submission and obedience is the natural result of *respect*, Cord."

His lean cheeks reddened. "Wow. How many more days do I have left to be schooled by you?"

"Only two."

"Praise God from whom all blessings flow, as we sang last night. Next time your boyfriend asks me to carry a message, I'll tell him to do it himself."

"I'd prefer it that way. Thank you." She gave him her sweetest smile.

He turned on his heel and his heavy footfalls sounded all the way along the upstairs hall and down the stairs.

All right, that hadn't been very *deemiedich* of her. He'd been right to call her on her lack of submission. But everything she'd said had been the truth. He just wasn't in the habit of hearing it.

Her gaze fell on her closet, which held her few dresses and aprons, but was mostly taken up with the deep shelving where she kept the quilts she made. Unlike herself, they were patient, simply waiting for her.

So the Amish Diamond had sold, and sixty percent of its price was hers. She ought to steel herself and choose one or two of these to take into town. They weren't doing any good sitting there in the dark.

There were six, two full-size and four queen size. Snow Goose, Winter Stars, Christmas Time—she had made these over the last two summers, when it was hot. Somehow the blues, silvers, and bare-tree browns of the first two made her feel cooler as she worked with them. She couldn't give up Winter Stars or Snow Goose yet. Not if there might be winter weddings on the Circle M.

She set aside Christmas Time for Rose, a happy mix of red, green, and white. It likely wouldn't sell when people's children were going back to school, but maybe during Thanksgiving it would.

The remaining three were a Blooming Nine-Patch called Roses she'd made for fun because it was a fast pattern that looked far more complicated than it was, an Irish chain she called Amish Chain because of its traditional colors, and another wreath—Daffodil Spring.

Roses and the Amish Chain joined Christmas Time. If the lady from Nevada had liked the purples, greens, and burgundy shades on black that were the colors of Amish dresses, then someone else might, too. And that was enough bidding farewell for one day. She slid the quilts into dry cleaning bags to protect them and glanced at the clock ticking cheerfully on the window sill.

Only three o'clock. She had time to hitch up Hester and take them into town.

She'd better do it quick, before she changed her mind and put them all back in the closet like Ebenezer Scrooge hoarding his gold.

12

ZACH HAPPENED to be in the barn and ambled out of the tack room to help her hitch up Hester. "Where are you headed off to? You could have gone with Cord earlier."

"*Neh, denki.* A little of Cord goes a long way. I'm taking some more quilts to Rose." She couldn't help a smile. "I shouldn't be so hard on our star boarder. He came upstairs to tell me the Amish Diamond quilt sold. Which was nice of him."

Zach's eyebrows rose in appreciation. "*Gut* news. Now I see why you want to take her another one ... or twelve."

"I only have these three to spare. They might not sell for months."

"I wouldn't be so quick to assume that." He patted Hester on the neck and walked her forward. "Hop in."

The five miles to town seemed to go by in moments. Malena actually had to quiet her thoughts—whirling with designs and time calculations and wondering if she had enough blue and purple on hand for Montana Lupine—to concentrate on driving. Hester might know the way well enough, but she'd have plenty of apologizing to do to the horse if she drove her right into the ditch, like Cord and his big truck.

There were no empty parking spaces in front of the shop, or in front of the bookstore or the dress shop, either. Without a hitching rail on this side closer than the bank, she made a left turn into the tiny parking lot of the smithy, where at least the rail was empty, even if the car spots were occupied. She hoped Alden wouldn't mind, but she'd only be a minute.

It was a bit of a struggle to wrestle the bulky bags plus her handbag across the highway. When she pushed into the quilt shop, a bead of sweat ran down from her hairline to her chin.

"Malena," Rose said in surprise, looking up from the cutting table, where a customer stood. "Did Cord tell you the Amish Diamond sold?"

"That's why I'm here." She heaved the bags onto the sales counter. "I brought more." Then a thought struck her like a blast of cold wind. "Oh—I'm sorry—I should have asked first." Heat burned into her cheeks as the customer's curious gaze fell on the bags. "I shouldn't have assumed—the other quilts should have their time in the window."

Rose was already shaking her head. "If you hadn't, I might have asked Alden to drive out to the Circle M tonight and sweet-talk you out of them. Here you go," she said to her customer. "Two and a half yards of the strawberry polka dot. The thread is right over there, and you might pick out some white bias tape to make trim. Your little girl will look wonderful on her first day of school."

The lady took the fabric absentmindedly. "Are you going to take those out of the bags? Can I see?"

"Of course," Rose said easily. "Maybe you could help us choose the one to go in the window."

"Me? Oh, I'd love to. I'm so glad I talked my husband into

buying the kids those big cookies at the café so I could get some time to myself. What do you call those?"

"Whoopie pies," Malena supplied. "My favorite are the pumpkin cream cheese. But Ellie, the café owner, says I have to wait until October."

"My kids are probably cleaning them out of the chocolate ones and..." Her voice trailed away as Rose shook out Roses and put it on the display bed, then did the same with Amish Chain. "Oh my. Is this your work?" she asked Malena. She touched the stitching with reverence.

"The piecing is," she said honestly. "It's a traditional pattern. My mother and sister, and my brother's fiancée help with the quilting."

"Look at that." With her finger, the woman traced the feathered border, then the wheels of feathers on the plain black blocks between the chains. "It's beautiful. How much are you asking for it?"

Rose glanced up at Malena, who had lost the power of speech. "There is more piecing than the Diamond, but less quilt stitching overall. Shall I split the difference, and ask the same?"

Malena could only nod.

"Eight hundred," Rose told the customer, in the same pleasant tone as she'd recommended bias tape. "We take cash or checks, but not credit cards, I'm afraid. We're not online here."

Malena braced herself against the counter to keep from falling over. Eight hundred dollars! How could Rose say it straight out like that and not stammer at her own daring?

The woman nodded. "I'll just run across the road and check with my husband. It's either this or some fancy rifle for our Montana souvenir, and I'll tell you which one *I* want the most in our bedroom."

She laid the polka dots on the counter next to the cash register and hurried out.

Malena had to breathe deeply before she could speak. "You got *eight hundred dollars* for the Amish Diamond?"

"I did," Rose said. "And you owe me a cupcake. You didn't think the Glacier Lily would sell for fifteen, and it fetched two thousand."

"Don't remind me," Malena groaned. "Poor Alden is never going to hear the end of it."

"He has broad shoulders," Rose said with a smile. "If that customer comes back with her husband's approval, maybe I can pay you for both."

The lady did, beaming broadly, and with cash to boot. "You can buy a wrought-iron quilt rack at the blacksmith's shop across the way," Rose said. "My son makes them."

"Oh no," the customer said happily. "This is going on our bed. Thank you so much." The large bag filling her arms, she headed back to the café, where presumably the family car was parked.

Other than her share of the cattle money in the autumn, Malena had never in her life earned this much money in so short a time. Rose carefully counted out the bills and handed them over. "Sixty percent of eight hundred, twice."

"You take the sixty on this one," Malena begged. "Please. I don't feel right taking so much."

"You reap what you sew," Rose told her with a grin. "And I'd like a red velvet cupcake with cream cheese frosting, *bidde*."

Malena didn't dare walk down the street with so much money. She went to the bank and deposited it, saving out a little to buy Rose and her family half a dozen cupcakes, as well as some fabric for herself. And by the time all her transactions were completed, Roses was hanging in the shop window, Christmas Time was set to take its place on the first of November, and Mountain Home's stores and the Bitterroot Dutch Café were closing up.

"Come home with us for dinner," Rose urged. "This calls for a celebration."

She hadn't seen Alden all afternoon. And maybe there was a teensy part of her that had driven to town for just that purpose. That had been waiting for him to walk across the highway every minute since she'd so blatantly tied up her horse in his parking lot.

"I'd like that," she said. "Can I use your phone? Someone will hear it ring in the barn."

Zach, true to form, was still there. She asked him to tell Mamm she wouldn't be back for dinner. "We want to celebrate tonight, *Bruder*—I hadn't even got the Amish Chain in the window when an *Englisch* lady bought it."

"Well done." She could practically hear his smile. "I'll share the news, and take special care to let Cord know you're eating with your boyfriend's family."

"You do that. *Denki*."

Dat didn't like his *Kinner* being on the phone too long. If it wasn't ranch business, any topic of conversation could be dealt with in five minutes or less. And she had better not tie up Rose's business phone, either. She hung up, and waited outside for Rose to close the shop.

Alden's smile broadened into a grin when he turned from locking up the smithy to see her and his mother crossing the little parking lot together.

"Hallo," he said. "I'd say this was a nice surprise, except that Hester gave it away."

"Here's the surprise," Rose said. "She's coming home with us for dinner."

"*Neh*, you're going home with me," Malena teased. "Alden, why don't you ask Hester if she minds you driving?"

Hester had no objections, and even if she had, it was a drive of only two minutes to their little house. The scent of hamburgers sizzling on the barbecue grill wafted across the backyard as Alden unhitched Hester and took her to their small barn.

"Oh my," Malena said. "Such a treat." She loved hamburgers—loaded up with cheese, lettuce and tomatoes from the garden, and fried onions and bacon. And gobs of blue cheese dressing.

Beth waved the spatula in greeting. "Onions?"

"The works," Malena called cheerfully. "And hi to you, too."

"*Gut* to see you, Malena. We got the white cheddar the Zook brothers made in the spring," Julie added. "Cheddar-burgers!"

"*Wunderbaar!*"

It had been a fair while since Malena had been out for dinner on her own, without the entire family—or at least her brothers and twin—and outside of church or singing. It was something that courting couples did. Things hadn't ever progressed to that point with the other boys she'd dated. She didn't have an older sister to confirm it, but she'd heard that a girl might have to field a few discreet questions to see if she would be a good match for son and brother, casual inquiries and hints about hope chests included.

Not so at the Stolzfus backyard picnic table. Because

nothing said *family* like blue cheese dressing dripping down your chin, or waving a home fry covered in ketchup to make a point in lively conversation. It was so tempting to take refuge in talking about quilts with Rose. Quilts were Malena's safe place. But she was learning that Alden's home could be that, too.

So instead of covering up her shyness by being boisterous, laughing and cracking jokes, she helped the conversation flow instead to the family's move out here. To asking Rose about differences in communities and adjusting to a new *Ordnung*. To gently discovering why Julie loved hockey: "It reminds me of my grandfather before he died. He loved it, too. Played in goal, right up until he was seventy." And why Beth liked to experiment in the kitchen: "In Colorado they put together a cookbook for the tourists to buy, every woman contributing a favorite. Rexford did the same. I wondered if we might do that here, since we're getting more tourists every year."

"*Gut* idea, *Schweschder*," Alden said. "Every Amish shop could sell them, and you could have a table at the auction next year."

He was so smart. "All the proceeds could go to the school, or into the medical fund," Malena suggested.

She was almost sorry when the food was gone, the conversation had been so interesting. Rose and her daughters told her she was their guest and they'd clear up, and to sit herself down while they brought out dessert.

Which left her alone with Alden for a few minutes.

"I think they did that on purpose." He smiled across the table. "My family is not known for being subtle."

"Neither is mine," she said with a twinkle. "But you have to admit, plain speaking gets the job done. By the way, *denki* for letting Hester and me take up space in your parking lot today."

The smile broadened, that long dimple creasing his cheek. "I was glad. It meant that you'd have to come back, and then I could spring out of my lair and catch you."

Before she could decide if he was teasing or serious, her mouth ran away with her. "Rumor has it you did that already."

Instead of the laugh she expected, that dimple faded. "I told Mamm and the girls that this is just temporary."

"You did right. I don't want to lie to our families."

"Even if we're lying to the *Gmee?*"

She was silent, trying to put the right words in order on her tongue. But to her own dismay, she lost control of that unruly member and out it came. "What if we ... weren't?" Then she blushed scarlet. Oh dear, she should never have said that out loud. "I mean—that is—"

What on earth was wrong with her tonight?

"Are you saying ... that you want a real courtship?"

His eyes had widened. His face had gone slack.

And she realized the magnitude of her mistake.

Before she could get out a single word, the door opened and Rose and his sisters trooped down the stairs with a round three-layer cake, plates, and a tub of ice cream.

"*Hallich Geburtsdaag*, Alden!"

Beth and Julie sang the birthday song in *Englisch* while Malena did her best to sing along. She had not known it was his birthday today. But then, before this week, she hadn't known much about him at all. And now, he knew the worst about her.

That she spoke without thinking.

That she was forward and unwomanly, asking a man to date her instead of waiting to be asked—and not just once, either. Twice.

That she was the last girl a man like him would want for a special friend, never mind a wife.

"Our *Bruder* is twenty-four today," Julie announced. "German chocolate is his favorite."

She served him a luscious slice of cake, glistening with caramel coconut pecan frosting on top and between the layers, with a scoop of vanilla ice cream. It was one of Malena's favorites, too—a girl with a waistline like hers obviously had quite a few favorites. If she hadn't just asked the most embarrassing question in the world, she would have savored every mouthful. As it was, she focused on the cake and let Alden's family reminisce about birthdays past.

Maybe he'd forget what she said, under all the talk and banter. Maybe she could go in and start on the dishes. Maybe he'd been so shocked by her asking him to court her for real that he'd never want to see her again.

The dishes. *Ja*. That was the best plan.

She scooped up her empty plate and Julie's, too.

"Malena, you don't have to do that. You're our guest."

"I'm just saying *denki*," she said with her best impression of a smile, and escaped into the house.

She managed to stay in the kitchen, up to her elbows in soapsuds, despite the protests of Beth and Julie. It was easier when you were the one doing the washing—once you were wet, sensible people let you stay there and finish the job. Sadly, hamburgers meant there weren't big pots or casserole dishes to scrub, which would have given her a good reason to stay longer at the sink.

To her enormous relief, Alden had gone somewhere when darkness fell and she said her good-byes and thank-yous to his family. She escaped across the lawn to the barn and slipped inside, where some considerate person had left a Coleman lamp burning.

"Come on, Hester, time to run away."

Hester whickered, and one ear swiveled to the left.

"Run away from what?" Alden stepped out of the darkness and into the pool of light.

❧ 13 ❧

ALDEN HAD BEEN in the barn only a few minutes—long enough to light the lamp for Malena and tidy up a little before she came out. Long enough to panic about what he would say to her when she finally did appear.

Because it was clear that something had gone very wrong just before his sisters had brought out the birthday cake. What it was, he didn't know, but he had the chilling feeling that it was because he'd been so forward. Daring to think that they might have a real courtship, not just a two-week rehearsal.

She must have meant something else, and he'd misunderstood. Because he'd barely heard another word from her during dessert, and she'd escaped into the kitchen to prevent a cozy chat at the picnic table.

He had to make it right. And if ambushing her in the barn was his only option, why then, he'd take it.

Especially after she'd said she wanted to run away.

At his words she whirled, and Hester sidestepped, startled at the sudden movement.

"Or maybe I should say, run away from who?" he went on.

"Alden. You scared me."

"Sorry," he said. He really was. No man wanted to see that horrified expression on the face of the woman he dreamed about. "Malena ... don't run away. Can we talk a little?"

She nibbled the inside of her cheek. "I really should go. It's dark, and my folks will be worried."

"I don't need long to say my piece. Only as long as it takes to help you hitch up Hester." He held out a hand for the leading rein, and nearly sighed with relief when she gave it to him. Hester walked beside him over to the slats of the buggy, then let him back her between them. Facing each other over the horse's back, they began to fasten buckles.

He had to get his thoughts to solidify into words. Buckles were good for keeping the hands busy, but they only took a few minutes.

"I want to know if you meant it, Malena. About ... what you said."

Her back was to the lamp, her face in shadow. His face, on the other hand, had no defense. Everything he felt was right there, the truth illuminated for her to see.

"I say all kinds of things. Mostly nonsense."

"Was it nonsense about ... us courting for real?"

"I didn't mean to be so forward—you must think I—"

"What I think is ... I wish it *was* real."

She went still. "You do?"

"If you do." When she didn't speak, the words filled him up until he had to get them out. "I want to court you. Not just to keep Cord McLean out of your hair, but for ourselves. To get to know each other. To find out what we have in common. And what we don't."

"I like German chocolate cake, too," she offered, after a moment.

ADINA SENFT

He couldn't help his smile at the unusual sight of Malena Miller suffering from a bout of shyness. Usually he was the one being awkward and tongue-tied. "That's a start. And I think your quilts are a gift from *Gott*."

"They are."

"There now, see? That's a *gut* beginning."

She moved, and the light struck her face, showing him the heart-shaped outline of cheek and chin. She was so beautiful it squeezed all the breath out of his lungs.

"All right," she whispered. Her hands fell away from the harness.

In the time it had taken to hitch up a horse, the whole course of his life changed.

"Gut," he managed. "I'm glad." He blew out a breath. "That was the hardest thing I've ever done."

Her bubbling laugh made him smile, too, in spite of himself.

"I thought for sure and certain you would think I was forward—pushy even," she said. "I was so ashamed of myself I ran away into the kitchen."

"You weren't forward," he assured her. "Plain speaking, remember? It's risky, I know. No man wants to lay his feelings out, only to have someone laugh at him. Or worse, tell all her buddy bunch so *they* can laugh at him."

"No woman worth having feelings for would do that."

"You'd be surprised. There was a *Maedsche*—" He shook his head, surprised to find that the acutely embarrassing memory had faded into just a story that he might tell her one day. Or he might not. "All behind us. From this moment on, the past doesn't matter."

"Agreed. Not that I have any kind of a past. I've only dated

152

a couple of boys," she confessed. "The others were just friends."

He stifled his curiosity to know who they were. She'd lived here all her life, so he might know them. But *neh*. It wasn't important. Because he was her special friend now, for sure and certain, and nobody else mattered.

"I should get home," she said, moving back to the driver's side. "See you tomorrow?"

He couldn't help making a face as he slid Hester's reins through their channels in the wind screen. When she gathered them up, he said, "I'll be at the Rocking Diamond tomorrow and probably Wednesday. Doc MacDonald and I are shoeing their second string of trail horses."

"That's a big job. But you'll be glad of the pay."

"I am. I'm half tempted to offer Cord a lesson in shoeing, just so he's off the Circle M for a while. It'd be a sacrifice, but for you, I'd do it."

"Oh, could you?" She half turned in her seat as he stood by her door. "Even if it's only an hour. Honestly, Alden, I'll be so glad when he's out of the valley for good."

He'd only been half kidding, because teaching Cord McLean anything was bound to be a chore, but the relief in her voice decided him. "Maybe you could give him the message at breakfast, then. Doc and I plan to meet at the gates at seven, and get as much done as we can before it gets too hot."

"I will. *Denki*, Alden. If I can get Cord to go, I hope he won't be too much of a bother."

"If he gets out of line, Doc will deal with him. He doesn't suffer fools gladly."

She chuckled. "Or at all. Maybe that's why he and Dat get along so well."

He couldn't see her face in the darkness, until he reached in and turned on the buggy lamps. "*Guder nacht*, then, Malena."

"*Guder nacht.*"

Sitting in the buggy, her face was about level with his. Any other man would try to steal a kiss. But this was all so new, so miraculous ... It seemed to him that their budding feelings ought to be handled the way you'd handle baby chicks. Carefully, conscious of their fragility.

"I want you to know..." he began.

"*Ja?*"

"I want to kiss you, but this feels so new I don't want to ... mishandle it. Us."

"Your wanting to is enough for now," she said softly. "We're in no hurry, are we?"

"*Neh.*" He could wait a little.

He stepped out of her way, and she shook the reins over the horse's back. The sound under the wheels drifted back to him, changing from crunching gravel in their yard to the harder, less noisy sound of the asphalt on the street. Then it faded altogether.

No, the moment he kissed Malena Miller would be special. Romantic. Unforgettable. Not with her in a buggy and him in a barn.

MALENA WAS A *GUT* DRIVER, BUT NAOMI KNEW THAT HORSES could sometimes be frightened, and buggies were fragile compared to a truck or car. So her body relaxed with relief when the buggy lamps glimmered through the trees, and she heard the clip-clop of Hester's hooves coming up the lane.

Deborah turned her head away from the breast and Naomi

had a few minutes to set herself to rights and burp her before she heard Malena's firm step on the rear deck and the kitchen door opened.

"I'm in here, *Liewi*," Naomi called softly as Deborah settled against her chest.

Malena came to stand in the doorway, taking in her tiny sister's face in the light of the single lamp. "Is she asleep?"

"I won't be far behind. Did you have a nice time?"

Malena nodded, and the dreamy curve of her smile made Naomi's motherly instincts sit back with contentment, like a cat who has just finished a saucer of milk.

"I'll get us a snack, shall I?"

Which seemed to indicate her daughter wanted a quiet talk. "Becca made a batch of lemon-lime coconut cookies. You might find one or two left." Noah had come over for supper, hence the experimentation with the flavors he liked. And no one in the family was complaining—not even their star boarder.

In a few minutes, Malena came in bearing a tray on which were two mugs of warm milk and honey, and a couple of cookies.

"We are breaking down Cord's principles one at a time," Naomi reported, savoring the tang on her tongue. "He ate one of these with barely a protest."

"He has principles?" Malena asked with mock surprise.

"When it comes to his work, I suppose he does. The rest of them are none of our business." Naomi paused. "Except when it comes to you, that is."

Malena buried her nose in her mug. When she surfaced, that dreamy look was back. "Alden and I had a talk just before I left. While he helped me hitch up."

"Oh?" Naomi adjusted the sleeping weight of the baby in her arms.

"No more pretend. He asked if we could court for real."

Naomi tried to look interested, not delighted. "And what did you say?"

Color seeped into her cheeks. "It was hard for me not to think that I—that he—that I'd misunderstood somehow. I didn't want him to think I was being forward. He didn't want me to think *he* was. In the end we finally managed to ask each other if we could be special friends."

Naomi had never understood what it was in her outgoing, life-of-the-gathering daughter that had taught her not to believe in herself. Could it have been something in Naomi's upbringing? The very thought horrified her. Humility was something they all sought. But not this. Rebecca had been brought up just the same way, and she was just as shy and doubtful of herself. Was it being the only girls in a family of boys for so long? Or was something deeper going on?

"*Dochsder*, can you tell me why you might have thought you'd misunderstood, or he didn't mean it?"

"I don't know." She finished up the last bite of the cookie. "Everyone thinks I'm too loud—that I laugh too much. Take up too much space."

"I don't think anyone believes that now that we have a movie star in residence. You look like a pink prairie smoke flower in comparison."

"Hiding in a meadow, hoping not to be noticed?"

"Something like that."

"But he'll go away eventually, and people will think what they think." Malena set her empty mug on the tray.

"*Liewi*, no one thinks you're *hochmut* or greedy for attention."

"Mammi Glick did."

A tingle of shock ran through Naomi at the mention of her mother, dead now for several years. Deborah opened one eye, as if to ask why her arms had gone suddenly stiff.

"Tell me," Naomi said softly, relaxing her hold deliberately.

Malena sat back, her gaze distant as she found her way into the past. "We had just started school, so we were maybe six or seven? She came to visit and we took her up to see Grossmammi's orchard."

"I remember that visit." Sharon Glick had always been brisk and businesslike, and not given to overflowing emotion. At Naomi's wedding to a man she liked and respected, she had smiled, but not the kind that made you smile in return. As she aged, she had ... well, if her mother were an apple and emotion its juice, Naomi would say she had dried out. Maybe her marriage to Dat, who couldn't seem to succeed at anything, even living for very long, had been part of it.

And maybe Naomi had better stop criticizing her mother in her thoughts. It would profit her nothing, and keep Deborah from sliding back into sleep. She did her best to relax both mind and body this time.

"Becca and I were running from one tree to another, so happy because it had been a long winter and the trees had finally bloomed. It was like a paradise in the canyon, white with blossom and smelling so sweet. It was like a gift we could give her."

"And ...?"

"And Mammi told us we were being too noisy. That running and screaming and laughing was unbecoming to Amish girls. That drawing so much attention was a sin, and we should be ashamed."

A spurt of anger flashed through Naomi's chest. Luckily

Deborah had fallen asleep once more, and wasn't nursing, or her milk would probably have curdled.

"She used to tell me that, too."

"Well, it was the first time Becca and I had been told so. We didn't know what to do."

"I'm sorry it spoiled your joy in the orchard. Grossmammi Miller would have been so sad."

"Something seemed to happen to us. Every time we made a noise, or laughed, or cracked a joke, we'd look at each other and feel guilty. Especially in front of the *Gmee*. We wondered if we really were bringing shame on the family."

"I hope you realized that you weren't."

"It takes some growing up to figure that out. Eventually I realized that laughter is a gift from *Gott*, as long as it's not directed against someone. And while Becca is more thoughtful than I am and people tend not to see her, she can laugh and run with the best of them."

Carefully, Naomi said, "Do you think what Mammi Glick said made Becca turn invisible?" Her quiet daughter had the uncanny ability to practically vanish in plain sight. But that was changing now that Noah could find her at a glance and somehow communicate to her that he loved the sight.

Malena thought the question over. "Maybe in the beginning. But honestly, Mamm, I think Becca likes not being noticed. She's an observer, always trying to figure people out. Maybe that's why she understands them better than I do. She takes the time to look."

"That will stand her in good stead as a mother, trying to figure out who broke the good candy dish."

Malena made a guilty face. "I gave you a pretty glass one for Christmas that year, out of my own cattle money."

"I know you did." How she loved this glowing, beautiful

daughter of hers! She was so like Naomi herself had been—not in looks, but in personality. "All I can say is that I understand. Mammi Glick had a hard life, and so, she was not exactly on speaking terms with joy. But *Dochsder*, never fear that your joy in the world and the people our *Gott* created is something to be ashamed of. It's a gift from Him. A gift, I think, that Alden appreciates."

"Do you know what he told me?" Malena looked down, her skin rosy in the lamplight. "He said there was something about me that draws people, like a fire on a cold day."

Naomi's regard for Alden Stolzfus multiplied about a dozen times. "He's right. *Gott* gave you fiery hair for a reason, *nix*? People like to be around you. Not because you're there for their entertainment, but because it delights you to be with them. It shows in your face, your eyes. It's a *wunderbaar* gift, one I've loved and appreciated many a time."

"You never said," she said softly.

"I should have before, so I'm saying it now. You and Becca are my heart's delight. So very different—one who charges into life, and one who stands back to reflect on it. And yet you share this gift. People want to be around you because you give of yourselves. You don't simply take. You make people comfortable, each in your own way."

"The way you do."

"I have to work at it," Naomi admitted. "You do it more naturally. Never be ashamed of that. Mammi Glick didn't know *everything*."

Malena laughed. "Spoken like the fourteen-year-old you used to be."

"Oh, she's still in there." Smiling, Naomi gazed down at Deborah. "I hope your little *Schwescher* will share that gift, too."

Malena leaned over to kiss the sleeping *Boppli.* "You're her mother. I think she will. So ... do you approve of my dating Alden?"

Naomi simply nodded. No words need be said that her daughter didn't already know.

And when Malena took the empty tray out to the kitchen, she was smiling as though she'd been given a present she couldn't wait to unwrap.

14

BREAKFAST WAS AT FIVE A.M., so that Dat and her brothers could do chores and make the rounds of checking the cattle in the home fields before they headed out to ride fence or do whatever was next on the unending list of repairs, improvements, and maintenance on the ranch.

Rebecca brought over a platter of bacon and sausage, and Sara followed with cheese biscuits made in Mamm's big cast-iron frying pan. Malena set a stack of purple blackberry pancakes on the table in front of Cord McLean, whose eyes didn't usually open properly until he was on his second cup of coffee.

"Alden Stolzfus and Doc MacDonald are going to be shoeing a string of horses on the Rocking Diamond today," she informed him cheerfully. "Alden says that if you like, he can teach you a little about farrier work. They plan to be there at seven."

Bleary eyes dropped to the expensive watch on his wrist. She had no idea which of its three dials actually told him the time. "Won't get the sluices done by then."

Joshua schooled his face to helpfulness. "That's okay, Cord. We can manage. It's probably more important for your role that you know some about shoeing."

Zach nodded. "There may not be sluices in your movie, but for sure and certain there will be horses."

Cord gulped his coffee—black, no sugar—and when he emerged from his mug, he looked as relieved as Malena's brothers. "Thanks, guys. I appreciate you cutting me some slack."

"Evening chores will still need to be done," Dat said, his morning voice unconsciously like a growl. At least, she thought it was unconsciously.

"I'll be back before then," Cord assured him. "I'll just pick up a few tips and maybe try that hoof-between-the-knees trick. That should be enough for filming."

Malena couldn't imagine that tricks and tips would fool an audience, but what did she know? Farriers apprenticed for several years before they hung out their own shingle, and Alden was learning what he could about livestock medicine from Doc MacDonald on top of that.

Relief that Cord would be gone for a good part of the day made her more relaxed than she usually was around him, and when he finally departed, she even gave him a wave as she took the scraps and crushed eggshells out to the aviary in the barn for the chickens. He was hoofing it up the track that made a shortcut between the two properties much faster than he ever walked down to the barn and out to the irrigation ditches.

Malena stifled a smile as she fed and watered the hens, then opened the door to the field they shared with the horses, where they hunted bugs and seeds. When she returned to the house, she found Sara putting on her black away bonnet.

"Want to come with me to the hay farm? They're coming

to install the new propane tank and hook up the gas stove and hot water tank." She smiled at the thought. "The last big job before I can move in and get the *Haus* ready for October."

"It's only August," Malena teased.

"Says the woman who doesn't have to make curtains for a dozen windows. My mother's sewing machine won't have been this busy since she—" Sara looked away.

Malena gave her a gentle squeeze. "Only one half of the window," she said, trying to be encouraging. "Your mamm made hers, too, when she was married, didn't she? It must have seemed like only half the work compared to where she came from." Their *Ordnung* permitted curtains in windows, but two was fancy. So one was extra wide so it could be drawn across, and during the day held back by a simple cord. "And don't forget we'll be making window quilts once you're back from your honeymoon trip."

While Amish houses in Montana had dual- and triple-paned windows, window quilts hung inside the frame to absorb the cold that still tended to seep through. They were a welcome addition to any house, especially on the north side, where the wind came howling down from Canada and every bit of protection counted.

"So do you want to come?" Sara had learned to embrace the happy side of her memories and step forward into her life.

"I'll come and help you sew next week," Malena promised. "Today I'm going to accept the gift of a certain someone's absence and work on a quilt design."

Sara laughed, picked up Nathan in his car seat with one hand and a picnic lunch with the other, and made her way down the steps. Joshua had already hitched up Hester and was waiting for his fiancée to head out before he joined Zach in the fields.

What she hadn't told Sara was that she and Rebecca had already measured all the farmhouse's windows, and Rebecca was making window quilts for the north side as her wedding gift. They were a sober blue, just like all the curtains in their district, but the quilted designs of the flowers found in the Siksika Valley made them special. Their sewing circle had made window quilts for the King house this spring, and Rebecca had used that big project as cover for the gift she already had planned for Joshua and Sara.

As for Malena's wedding gift to her youngest brother, it was time to get moving on it. She would not think about Montana Lupine just now. It could cook in the back of her mind while she worked on a design that was already completed. Several hours later she had a stack of triangles and diamonds that would eventually form a background similar to the one in Glacier Lily, with a floral shape that would only become visible when you stepped away and looked at it in its entirety. It had been a good day's work, only interrupted by a pick-up lunch just among themselves.

The big kitchen table was half empty—no Daniel now, no Joshua and Sara, no Adam—but all the same, she'd never complain about being with the people she loved most, with no strangers to have to explain things to every five minutes.

"I wonder how Alden is doing with his student?" Mamm said as she made herself a second roast beef sandwich slathered in horseradish and layered with lettuce and tomato from the garden.

Trust Mamm to ask the question Malena was wondering herself.

"I'm sure we'll hear all about it," Zach said. "Malena, I meant to tell you—if you wanted to give Cord a refresher on flycasting before tomorrow, I put a reel on the five-weight and stuck a couple of caddises in the handle for you."

What a sweetheart he was! She was half tempted to go around to all the girls in the district and tell them they were missing out on a wonderful man. But Zach probably wouldn't speak to her for the rest of her life if she horned in on his business like that.

"Denki, Bruder," she said instead. "That was kind of you. But Cord can probably give himself a refresher without my help."

"I think you'll find that boy doesn't do anything without an audience."

Truer words were never spoken.

Late that afternoon, when Cord returned to the Circle M, and Mamm suggested he practice casting before supper, the first words out of his mouth were an invitation for Malena to join him. All her reasons to refuse—finishing up her cutting, helping with the housework, starting dinner—went past his ears like a summer breeze. Oh, he was good at pleading. And she had to admit, getting rid of him for all those hours so she could have the happiness of work made her feel a little guilty for enjoying his absence so much.

"Fine," she said at last. "But only until you're comfortable with casting again. Did you get your gear out of your truck?"

"I did," he said happily. "Let's go."

Rods in hand, the two of them made their way down the river path to the big curve where there was a gravel bar and a couple of deep pools.

"I'll start over there," she said, pointing at the upstream end. "You might have good luck at this riffle down here, where that creek comes in."

He looked puzzled. "Then I'd have to holler at you to talk."

"Why would you want to talk?" The point of fly fishing was

the fish, of course, but also the restfulness of the spirit from being out in *Gott*'s creation. Listening to the river chatter with the birds. Seeing the wind blowing where it listed, and hearing the sound thereof.

"To tell you about my day." He looked at her as if this was obvious.

"What about *my* day?"

"What about it? What did you do while I was gone?"

"I cut out the background triangles and diamonds and curved pieces for the quilt I'm making Joshua and Sara for their wedding. I'm using pale gold, and green, and sky blue from our dresses, and a really pretty taupe for contrast, and it will have a—"

"When's the wedding?"

Why ask her what she'd done today and then cut her off in the middle of the telling? "October."

"It's August."

"A wedding quilt takes a lot of work and planning. And you have to start early, so there's time for a quilting frolic or two. That's when we get the stitching completed."

"Sounds ... fun." His voice was flat.

She couldn't resist. "Oh, it is," she said brightly, as though he'd really meant it. "But I had quite a time deciding whether to use green for the primary background, or whether the blue was the best contrast with the central—"

"Malena. Aren't you going to ask me about my day?"

It was a woman's place to give place. To be humble and obedient. And it wasn't that she thought her words had any more value than his. But she was really beginning to feel annoyed with his asking for them, and then cutting her off when she offered them. "You said—"

"I know. But I spent a whole morning with your boyfriend. Don't you want to hear about that?"

"No. I'm sure he'll tell me all about it. Right now I want to fish. And if you don't want to look as rusty as you say you are, you should, too."

And with that, she walked away across the gravel bar.

She wasn't losing her temper. She was just keeping him focused. All the same, it took several deep breaths before the calming sounds of the river had any power to soothe her ruffled temper.

Before she could even finish tying her fly to the tippet, here he was again. "I don't have any flies for this part of the country. They're all for California."

Wordlessly, she unhooked the second one on her rod's cork handle and held it out to him.

"Barbless?"

"*Ja*. We don't want to hurt the fish even if we land it."

"Are you mad at me?"

"No."

"You look mad. Did you break up with Alden or something?"

"No. But how would you feel if someone asked you to tell them about your day, about your work, and then interrupted you to talk about themselves instead?"

"Did I do that?" He sounded honestly mystified.

"Yes. Are you fishing or not?"

"I'm fishing. Give me some tips?"

"No, I'm busy."

"You *are* mad at me."

She took a deep breath, scented with the river and the sweetness of the wild roses nodding in a clump nearby. "Fly fishing is about you and the river. Go enjoy it. Tomorrow will be noisy and fun and you'll probably get wet and we'll all wind up swimming instead of catching enough for the fish fry. Take your opportunity while you can."

When he didn't move, she gave up and wet her finger, then held it up in the air.

"Wind's coming from the south, so our flies are going to blow back at us. Should we cross over or go up to the next bend?"

He gazed at the opposite bank. She was barefoot, but he wore jeans and his silly, expensive boots. Had he really been shoeing horses in those? "The next bend."

Carrying her rod, she led him down the path past the bench Dat had built for Mamm, to where the river curved just enough for the wind to carry a fly over the water. "It's not as good here, because we don't have that nice riffle, but something ought to bite."

There was no gravel bar here, only a grassy bank a couple of feet high. The grass felt good under her bare toes. She put half a dozen yards between them, set her creel down, and sent her fly across the water. She was a competent angler, but nothing like Kate Weaver, Adam's special friend. She and Adam were due back from Whinburg Township in a couple of weeks. She wished Cord could see Kate fish. She was so graceful and so absorbed in the art that it was like watching poetry.

Kate might even be engaged to her brother when they returned. How exciting that would be! If they were, maybe there would be three weddings on the Circle M. Mammi Miller always said that a house wasn't a home until it had seen a wedding, a birth, and a death.

Well, she could do without that last one. But Deborah certainly counted as the birth.

But with three wedd—

"I've never seen a woman look so pretty."

Malena nearly came out of her skin at the voice so close to her. "What on earth? I thought you were fishing."

"I got distracted." He was standing so near she could feel the heat coming off his body, as though he'd been working hard or running.

Neither of which had happened in the last half hour.

"You need to concentrate on your form," she told him.

"I was concentrating on yours."

A shiver of disgust ran through her. Was this how *Englisch* men flirted? Always bringing up the girl's body as if that was all that mattered? An Amish boy might appreciate a girl's figure, but he would never say so to her face. Be so forward about it.

"Was that a shiver?" His voice was caressing. "You can't be cold. What's making you shiver, Malena?"

"You know how you feel when you step in a meadow muffin and you lift your foot? It was that kind of shiver."

His eyes flashed before his lashes fell in what was clearly a practiced maneuver. "I think you're fooling yourself. I think you like me."

She was already reeling in her line. There would be no trout today. Without another word, she hooked the wet fly to the handle, and picked up her creel.

As she walked past him, he grabbed her arm. "Where are you going?"

"Back to the house."

"But I haven't even got my fly wet."

The fly she'd given him was stuck in the handle of his expensive-looking rod. She tried to shake him off, but he didn't let go. His hand slid to her wrist.

"You should stop wasting time," she said evenly. "Please let go."

"Are you this mean to Alden?"

"That's none of your business."

"Come on, Malena. Be nice. A million girls would—"

"She's not a million girls," said a calm male voice not ten feet away. Alden stood in the path gazing at Cord. "Reuben's looking for you."

The hand on her wrist loosened, and Malena jerked it out of his grasp.

"No, he's not," Cord said. "He knows I'm fishing."

"You can explain that to him when you go up. Or I could go back and mention you were bothering his daughter, and he'll kick you off the property. Your choice."

"Tell him whatever you want. Not that it's your business, but I've paid until Thursday morning."

As if the last five minutes had a price! As if money would excuse his behavior!

"This isn't a dude ranch," Alden pointed out, his tone even. "I think you'll find that to her dad, Malena's wellbeing is worth the loss of two hundred dollars."

With a hissed epithet, Cord flung his rod on the ground. Then he stomped past Alden and disappeared down the path, the violence of his language soon overcome by the rush of the water.

"Are you all right?" Alden picked up the abused rod.

"*Ja*, I'm fine." He didn't think she'd been encouraging Cord's behavior, did he?

"Seems our plan isn't working." He took the empty creel from her limp fingers and led her over to the river's edge. He sat on the grassy bank, his feet hanging over the edge, and invited her down beside him. "You should tell your father."

"I know," she said on a sigh. After a moment, she gave in to the need for comfort, and dared to lean on his shoulder. She'd never known something so simple could be so satisfying. "But it's only one more day. And everyone is coming tomorrow for the fishing frolic."

"I wonder what he thinks he'll gain by annoying you?"

A needle of cold pierced her stomach. "Alden, you don't think I *want* him coming around me, do you?"

He hesitated, then slid his fingers under hers where they rested on the grass. "*Neh*. Just the opposite."

Oh, how good his hand felt. So warm, and strong. Even the calluses told her how hard-working this hand was—how safe a woman would be with her hand in his. She entwined her fingers with his and for a moment, the two of them simply rested there in the sun, their hands discovering each other's contours for the first time.

"I've wanted a moment like this for weeks," he murmured at last, stroking her thumb gently.

"What a difference five minutes makes," she said in a wondering tone. "I told him his being near me was like stepping in a cow pie."

A chuckle rumbled low in his throat, then escaped in a full-bodied laugh. It was catching—she couldn't help laughing, too.

"I hope you don't feel that way about me," he said when he could speak.

"You know I don't," she said softly. "Being with you is like ... yellow flowers, and the first robin of spring, and sunshine."

He chuckled again, then sobered. "Really?"

"You said once that being with me was like a fire on a cold day."

"So I did. And I meant it. I feel it right now."

She leaned her head on his shoulder, a warm glow in her own heart. "I wish this moment could last forever."

"I do, too. But when this one ends, we can make another one. That's the good thing about moments."

"Isn't it *gut* that *der Herr* constructed time that way?"

He loved the way she thought. "I'm glad that this is *us* now. Real. Not pretend. It's like a miracle happened when I least expected it."

"I'm no miracle," she confessed. That was too hard to live up to. "I'm short-tempered sometimes. And I eat too much pie. Sleep so hard the house could burn down around me. And I can't master fried chicken no matter how many times Mamm shows me."

"Lucky thing I don't care for fried chicken."

She lifted her head to look at him in surprise.

"If it were the Miller elk stew, now, that might be a deal-breaker." His face was sober, but that long dimple was dying to make its presence known.

"You can rest easy, then," she said, tracing its outline down his cheek. "Both Becca and I can carry on the family tradition."

A little silence fell, one filled with quiet happiness and the sound of birds. The creatures had clearly decided that the noisiest threat had gone, and these two people dawdling on the riverbank meant them no harm. A pair of ducks paddled by, followed by a family of Canada geese, getting fat on grubs and river weed before they flew south for the winter.

"Do you think we should go back?" she asked dreamily.

"I think Cord has probably found out Reuben wasn't really looking for him. I'll have to ask *der Herr* to forgive my fib tonight when I say my prayers."

She chuckled. "Knowing Dat, the moment Cord stepped

into the barn he'll have given him a list of half a dozen chores. I think you're safe."

"Safe with you." He squeezed her hand.

Malena squeezed back. Never in her life had she known this kind of glowing happiness. It wasn't the kind that came with the safety and love of her family, though it had elements of that. It wasn't the kind she found among her quilts, though it came from within, too. No, it was a kind of happiness she'd never known before.

The kind that came with believing *Gott* had accomplished his purpose, and had sat back, smiling. As though He'd looked upon his work in bringing the two of them together, and had seen that it was *gut*.

15

ALDEN DROVE off the Circle M, he hugged close to himself the happiness of that half hour on the riverbank with Malena. But around those feelings fluttered shadows—misgivings, uncertainty. For he hadn't gone into the barn and quietly told Reuben about Cord's behavior. On the one hand, anything he said might smack of jealousy. Malena was perfectly safe in the house, surrounded by her family. But on the other hand, it stuck in his craw that Cord could get away with treating the woman Alden cared for like that.

She wanted to keep the peace. Cord would be gone the day after tomorrow.

But Alden's peace had taken a beating.

When he'd rounded that clump of willows and seen Cord pulling her toward him, despite her obvious unwillingness, it had been all he could do to stay calm. Did the actor believe that Amish girls were so inexperienced that they wouldn't know what he wanted? Had he somehow mistaken the open friendliness she showed everyone for encouragement? Or was she simply a little handy entertainment to break up the monotony of chores?

Alden would probably never know. But all the same, his worry about Malena's being within a hundred yards of the guy nagged at him, like a mosquito in a darkened room.

The next morning, he arrived at the Rocking Diamond to find Doc MacDonald in his pickup, studying the gates. "Fine job you did on these, Alden," he said in response to Alden's greeting. "I might have to hire you to make a pair for me."

"I'm afraid this is the limit of my skill," Alden said. "If you're looking for a bucking bronc or some pine trees done in wrought iron, you might have to look elsewhere."

Doc barked his short laugh. "I just need to keep coyotes— two- and four-footed—out of the yard," he said. "When my grandkids come over, they ought to be able to play out there without my daughter worrying they'll be carried off."

"I could probably manage that. I've got some time available after roundup."

"Good. I'll give you a call. For now, let's get the rest of these horses looked after. I'm glad the Madisons believe in regular trims and shoeing, but two days straight of the same thing isn't my favorite. I got into this job for the variety."

Alden drove through the gate, then got out of the wagon to close it behind Doc's pickup. The rest of the day was spent pretty much exactly as the previous one had been, trimming hoof after hoof and shoeing the ones who needed it. The only difference was that Alden didn't have to stop work to show Cord how to do things—or rather, how to look as though he were doing them. The actor had been more interested in photo opportunities to post to his Instagram account than in actually doing the work. Though to give him credit, he had a knack with a couple of these horses, at least, who allowed him to hold their feet between his knees long enough to get some actual instruction.

Without their aggravating student, he and Doc worked quickly and silently in the way two men did who were familiar with each other's routines. Each knew what the other would do next, and what equipment he'd need. Alden even got the opportunity to look at an abscess on the inside of one horse's knee. Doc stood aside to allow him to examine the animal, then discussed the pros and cons of their options for treatment. Alden treated the sore himself, and told Brock Madison he'd be over in a day or two to check on the animal.

When their day was done, Alden wrote up his hours for the invoice he'd send later for his services. Doc waved out the driver's window as Alden closed the gate behind them, and sped away to his dinner.

Alden flapped the reins over Joseph's back. "We're going to the Circle M, boy. I don't know about a fishing frolic, but a swim is going to feel mighty good."

It would also feel good to be on hand in case Cord forgot what he owed to the Miller family for putting up with him all week.

There were several buggies already lined up by the fence when he arrived—Cal Yoder's, his brother Dave's, and a number of their other friends. The sight of the Stolzfus buggy meant that Julie and Beth were already here, too. He unhitched Joseph and led him into the pasture where the other horses were grazing, then went around to dig his rod and flies out from under the seat of the farrier's wagon.

"Alden!" Malena and Rebecca emerged from the house, Cord on their heels. Which meant elation at seeing her again was quickly deflated by the reminder that the actor was under their roof for one more night.

The sound of buggies coming up the lane made him turn, and he understood the reason for the glad welcome in Rebecca's eyes. Noah King waved and backed his buggy into the space next to Alden's, his brother Simeon following in his own rig. Alden had a feeling that the passenger seat wouldn't be empty on the return trip. As though the sight had drawn her in, he could see Susan Bontrager's upright form striding across the fields in the distance.

Those two needed to fish or cut bait.

There had been a fishing frolic here every year since his family had moved here. Some years Alden and the girls had missed it, what with work and helping Mamm with the store and the house. But this year it was clear that nothing was keeping his sisters from another chance to see the actor that had been producing so many headlines lately in the local paper.

"Hi," Malena said a little shyly as she joined him at the door of his wagon. "I was hoping you'd come."

"I wouldn't miss it." He smiled into her eyes. "And I think you know why."

A flush rose in her cheeks and it was all he could do not to lean down and kiss her. But that would embarrass her in front of both family and friends, and he'd never subject her to that. But it seemed she saw the desire to do it in his face, for her blush deepened.

"All right, you lovebirds." Cord strolled up behind her and tapped her shoulder with the tip of his rod, as though he were a teacher with a ruler and she a misbehaving scholar. "None of that."

"None of what?" Zach appeared out of nowhere. "I didn't see anything. Did you, Ruby?"

Where had the bishop's daughter come from while he'd been gazing into Malena's sweet face?

"See what?" Ruby asked, her chocolate-dark eyes round and innocent.

Cord rolled his eyes. "Great. A Laurel and Hardy routine. I know when I'm outnumbered. See you on the river."

He loped off down the path, followed by Noah, Rebecca, and Zach.

"Who are Laurel and Hardy?" Ruby asked nobody in particular.

Nobody in particular could tell her.

"Come on." Malena touched his hand. "Let's go catch some fish. Becca and I made salads, and Ruby has been here all day, helping us with the baking."

"Chocolate pie," Ruby said happily. "And blackberry, and lemon meringue. We need something ridiculously bad for us after eating healthy fish and salad."

"And home fries," Malena reminded her. "Lots and lots of home fries, with salt and vinegar."

Alden's mouth was watering already, and he hadn't even cast a fly to provide his share of the meal.

Malena and Ruby had their rods and tackle ready, so he pulled off his work boots and socks and the three of them made their way down to the river. Alden greeted the *Youngie* as they passed, the girls mainly sticking to the bank and the gravel bar while the young men stood against the current. Nobody wore hip waders and proper boots with nonslip soles. Some had rolled up their pants. Calvin, of course, was out in the middle fully dressed, up to his thighs in water and blithely casting as though this were normal.

"I hope he's got another pair of pants," Malena said with a shake of her head, "or Mamm won't let him in the house."

"Where to?" Ruby asked. She glanced anxiously up the

path, where one of the Zook cousins from the valley's other church was striding toward them, his gaze on her.

"Let's go farther along," Malena suggested. "I have a favorite spot."

The glance she sent him from under her lashes told him exactly where it was, and a glow spread from his heart right out to his fingers.

Sadly, Cord was already there, casting with the rod Malena had rescued from the ground the night before. He was on the bank with Julie and Beth, making respectable S-curves in the air with his casts as though he hadn't a care in the world. Zach stood a little way upstream, out of reach of the barbless hook, craftily aiming his fly under the opposite bank with its long, bending grass, where trout sometimes hid.

Alden's sisters probably wouldn't thank him for setting up anywhere within earshot. If they'd intended to make Cord happy with their shy questions as they watched him fish, they'd succeeded. But now Alden felt as though he needed to watch out for their welfare, too.

Malena had taken it all in with one glance. "Come on," she said in a low tone. "It's shallow over there where Zach is. We can cross and fish directly opposite. If he tries anything, we can throw rocks at him."

Alden couldn't help but laugh. "More likely I'll fall in and look like a moose heaving myself up the bank to come to the rescue."

Her idea was *gut*. The bank wasn't nearly as well-trodden as the one opposite, the grass soft and springy under his feet. With every ounce of his being, he wished it were only he and Malena out here, fishing and talking about whatever came into their heads. But voices carried over the water, and Ruby had crossed with them, so he made do with simply enjoying the happy conversation of two young women who had known each other since birth.

Ruby even managed to make Zach feel better after a reckless trout jumped for his fly and it didn't set. "Try again," she called. "He's hungry."

Zach did, and within moments the trout hit the fly a second time. He reeled it in with the skill of long practice, and not only did Ruby applaud as he landed the fish, Julie and Beth did, too.

Alden snuck a look at Cord to see how he'd taken his audience's defection. Sure enough, the other man had pushed out his chest and with careless grace, sent his fly out so far it practically brushed Malena's nose. It was never going to catch a fish that way—

Something moved that shouldn't have. "Look out!" Alden shouted.

Under Cord's feet, on the edge of the three-foot bank, clods of dirt were falling away.

"The bank!" he called. "Back away—Julie, quick!"

Julie leaped back and where she had been standing, a clod tumbled into the water, but otherwise it remained stable.

Cord stayed where he was. "Sure, Stolzfus. Try to spoil my fun. I know you're—"

The bank collapsed with the suddenness and the silence of a distant avalanche. Cord's feet went out from under him, and with a shout, he landed in the river with a splash. The current grabbed him, ripped his rod from his hand, and sent it swirling away. Then it pushed him under a fallen tree.

Even from where he stood, horrified, Alden could hear the sound the actor's skull made as it struck the weathered, barkless trunk.

"Cord!" Malena shrieked.

Alden flung down his rod and plunged in. The water, frigid even in late summer, was the reason fishermen referred to fishing bare-legged as wearing "purple waders." Alden slogged across the river as fast as he could. By now Zach had seen the problem and was splashing toward him to help, but something wasn't right.

Instead of getting his feet under him and wading out, Cord seemed to be stuck, his head lolling, half submerged, and his arms paddling uselessly at the current.

Alden put everything he had into reaching him, at last plunging into the deeper trout pool under the tree's thick trunk. Two strong overhand strokes brought him next to Cord. He braced his bare feet against a submerged log and pulled him free of the long-dead branch that had stabbed through the man's shirt and held him fast, probably saving his life. If it hadn't, the current would have pushed him under the tree and held him below the surface against several year's worth of accumulated branches and detritus.

Cord's eyes rolled and tried to focus on Alden. He almost sounded drunk as he mumbled, "Are we swimming?"

Cold water would do that. Make your mouth stop working, freeze your thoughts, drain your ability to help yourself. He didn't have much time. Alden got both hands under his arms and tried to float him to the shallows, but his feet couldn't find the bottom. Cord was a dead weight.

"*Ich bin hier.*" Zach got an arm around Cord and Alden took the man's other side. Together, they pulled him over to shallower water, which was rippling over the freshly turned stones and already scouring away the chunks of the bank that had fallen in.

"Up on the solid part," Alden gasped. "Ready? One—two —heave."

Thank goodness the bank held. Julie and Beth grabbed Cord under the arms and dragged him out of harm's way while Alden and Zach climbed out, their clothes and hair streaming with water. The warm afternoon air felt like walking into a heated room.

"Is he all right?" Beth cried. "One minute he was fishing, the next he fell in."

"He hit his head," Alden said. What would have happened if the bank had given way while he and Malena were sitting here—with no one in earshot to come and help? He felt sick at the thought. "He got trapped in that sweeper. If a branch hadn't caught his shirt, he'd have been swept under it and might have drowned."

"Does that mean you saved my life, Stolzfus?" came an exhausted voice from behind them. Cord still lay on his back, staring at the sky. He tipped his head to meet Alden's gaze.

"God saved your life," Alden said shortly. "Can you sit up?"

Cord struggled to a sitting position, crossing his legs and burying his hands in the grass as though trying to hang on to a spinning earth.

"Sara's here." Malena jogged up—Alden hadn't even known she'd gone for help. Carrying her EMT backpack, Sara Fischer flung herself to her knees in front of the actor.

"See my finger?" She held it up in front of him. "Follow it."

Both eyes focused on the slender finger and followed it from side to side, then up and down. Sara took out a penlight next and shone it in his eyes. He flinched and blinked, but she only nodded. "What day is it?"

He looked puzzled. After a moment's thought, he said, "Wednesday?"

"What month?"

"August. It's Wednesday, the eighteenth of August. My trainer will be here tomorrow. The nineteenth."

She sat back on her heels. "Well, that's a relief. Can I touch your head?"

His lids drooped to half mast. "You can touch anything you want."

She rolled her eyes over her shoulder at Alden and Zach. "I think he's going to be fine." All the same, her hands were gentle as she examined his skull. "You've got a nice sized hematoma forming here. Malena said the bank collapsed and you went in. How'd you manage this?"

"I don't know."

Alden said, "The current sent him into that sweeper and he got clocked on the head. He was a bit disoriented when we pulled him out."

"I bet he was." She glanced downstream and took in what Alden had already seen. "That could have got ugly in a hurry." Then she turned back to her patient. "Do you think you can walk up to the house?"

"Sure."

But it took two tries to get him up. Sara frowned as he got his balance on the second try.

"I think you should go to the clinic in Mountain Home and get checked out. Your initial responses were good, but your balance worries me."

"I don't want an ambulance. I can drive."

Sara's laugh was short and humorless. "Absolutely not. I'll call the Madisons and get someone to come over. A truck will get you there sooner and more comfortably than a buggy, and the Madisons are big donors to that clinic. You'll be seen right away. Come on."

With Alden and Zach on either side in case he lost his

balance again, she followed her patient up the path. The *Youngie* turned to gaze in surprise, and Alden realized that only about ten minutes had passed. Ten minutes more saw Cord bundled into Taylor Madison's Mercedes SUV and borne off down the lane at a higher rate of speed than its gentle curves usually saw.

While Sara took her backpack into the house, Malena joined him. "You should change into some dry clothes."

He had been drying in the sun, and he wasn't uncomfortable. "No need," he said, taking her hand in his cool one. "I'm going to see if I can find his rod. It was a thousand-dollar Sage and the reel was probably half that. I wouldn't want to lose it if it were mine."

"Then I'll come with you. And we should let the others know to watch for it."

The path down to the river wasn't wide, but it seemed to be wide enough for them. He didn't want to embarrass her, so when they emerged from the willows onto the gravel bar, he let go. Strange how empty his hand felt at the loss of hers—as though it had lost its purpose. Which didn't make much sense when he made his living with his hands.

Gott had one more purpose for them, it seemed, that went beyond sense.

Malena called to everyone within earshot to be on the lookout for the rod. Then they retraced their steps to the grassy spot past the bench. His sisters and Ruby were gone.

"Zach must have gone to change," Malena said. "Like a sensible person." She grinned up at him.

"Not so sensible to get two pairs of pants wet," he pointed out. Then, unable to help himself, he gently touched one of her deep dimples with his forefinger.

To his surprise, she reached up and did the same to him.

Her fingertip on his cheek sent a thrill through him that was almost a shiver. "I've been wanting to do that for ages," she said.

"Me too." For far longer than she suspected. "But if we get distracted, the rod will only travel farther downstream."

Her nose wrinkled in a moue of distaste. "Cord is getting in the way again. He's so good at it he doesn't even need to be here."

"You heard what he said—his trainer is coming tomorrow. And I'll bet Taylor Madison won't allow him out of her sight now. If someone doesn't come for his stuff by suppertime, I'll be surprised."

"What a relief it will be to get back to normal, *nix*?" This time it was she who took his hand as they stood together, safely away from the unstable stretch of bank. "So, the rod. The current would have taken it out into the middle, then against that far bank. It's just soil, like it is here, so nothing would have stopped it."

"I can't see it," he agreed. "At least the cork handle will let it float for a while."

They moved on to the little clearing where the bench stood, and scanned the river together. Nothing caught Alden's attention. Nothing except Malena and the trusting way her hand fit in his, their fingers entwined.

It wasn't difficult to plot the likely course of the rod as the river carried it around its loops and bends. But that didn't mean they could catch up to it before the Siksika straightened out and headed around the distant shoulder of the mountain. If that happened, Cord would be out an expensive rod.

There was a shout, and Dave Yoder climbed the opposite bank, soaked to the thighs. He waved the rod over his head. "Got it! The hook was tangled in some weed down here."

And their few precious moments of holding hands were over, just like that.

It didn't take long before the in-possession limit of twelve trout was reached by the more serious among them. Dave, who had a practical mind, had been keeping track. The triumphant anglers made their way back to the house in twos and threes, some bearing fish big enough to eat, some simply having been content to enjoy a day outside with their friends and eat the catch for supper.

Alden was looking forward to fresh trout for dinner, along with all the other *gut* things the family had prepared. But he couldn't help but think that he'd go without all of it if he could only spend a few more minutes on the riverbank, alone with Malena.

16

NOBODY CAME for Cord's things that evening—not even for his valuable Sage rod. Once she'd stashed it in his room, Malena had forgotten about it. She hoped that the doctor at the clinic had found nothing seriously wrong after his encounter with the sweeper, but mostly he was pushed out of her mind by the reality of Alden.

They hadn't dared to sit together at supper, because the ribbing and teasing would have gotten out of hand, and she wasn't certain how pleased Dat would be by his daughter putting on such a public display. But her senses were so finely tuned to Alden that she could practically feel where he was, be it living room or kitchen, deck or steps. He seemed to be the same way—she had eaten at the picnic table outside, and there he was with one of his sisters, eating off the deck rail not six feet away. When the volleyball net was set up, somehow they wound up on the same side. And when he went out to the pasture to get his big horse, it was perfectly natural for her to be out there already to help.

It was almost like being an engaged couple, and permitted to be together openly.

Sort of.

At breakfast the next morning, she was dreamy and abstracted, remembering the day before and the touch of his strong blacksmith's fingers, so gentle on her skin. Dat had to say her name twice before she blinked and realized he had asked her a question.

"Since our house guest didn't come back for his belongings," her father repeated, "what do you suppose we ought to do with them, *Dochsder?*"

"He'll turn up sooner or later," she said, and went back to her eggs. They were her favorite, scrambled with lots of cheese, topped with fresh tomato salsa made with her aunt's chili peppers from New Mexico, and served over pan-fried potatoes.

"If anything, he'll have to come back for that rod and reel," Zach said. "I'm glad we found them. It's a nice outfit."

"I'm not comfortable with expensive toys like that in my house," Dat grumbled. "Malena, I want you to take his things over to the Rocking Diamond this morning. Then we'll be shed of him."

"Me? Dat, he has a mountain of luggage as well as that rod."

"Six bags," Zach clarified, his mouth full. He should know —he'd carried half of them up the stairs the week before.

"Good grief," their father said, clearly having not stuck his head into the guest room since their guest had arrived. "All right. Take the rod over so at least it's where it belongs. Then remind them someone needs to come get the other things. We can't spare Hester today. Your mother and Lovina have errands in town."

Malena sighed, and tried not to show it. Maybe she could run the errand quickly and go with them to town, too. Then she'd stop in at Rose Garden Quilts to see if Roses had sold. "All right. They're up by seven. I'll take it over then."

Seven o'clock found her with rod in hand, walking up the path to the meadow where Adam planned to build his house, and then over the hill via the shortcut they often used to get to the bishop's. It kept them off the shoulders of the highway, so that buggies could travel unimpeded. After that, it was only a quarter mile to the Rocking Diamond's gates.

Alden's beautiful gates. She paused a moment to admire his work, then recollected that Mamm and Lovina would probably leave the ranch around eight thirty, which didn't give her much time for daydreaming.

As she approached the Madison house, it struck her again how much it looked like a hotel. But it was none of her business. Her business was getting this rod back to its owner, and getting said owner moved off the Circle M.

Trey Madison answered the door. "Hey, Malena. Come on in."

She hesitated, then sidled over the threshold into a living room so big you could fit Daniel's entire house inside it. Enormous windows looked out on the neat pastures and fields belonging to the family. Hanging from the highest point of the ceiling, where thick vaulted beams met, was a chandelier made entirely of elk racks. Lamps the size of dinner plates hung from it in a cascade. She no longer had any trouble believing the place had eight bathrooms.

"What can we do for you?" Trey asked. "Going fishing?"

She recalled herself to her errand. Holding out the rod, she said, "Cord lost this in the river yesterday when he fell in. It doesn't seem any the worse for wear, luckily. Can you give it to him?"

He took it, checking the fly stuck in the handle the way anglers did. "Sure. He's here. Do you want to see him?"

"He's back from the clinic?"

Trey nodded. "Last night. They couldn't find anything wrong with his balance or his ears, and there were no signs of concussion, so they sent him home. My mom says thank you for having him checked out, though."

"Oh, Malena is always checking me out." The familiar lazy voice came from the other side of the room, where a wide hallway presumably led to the guest rooms. "My little ray of sunshine. She can't stay away."

"I brought your rod and reel back," she said, determined to ignore his nonsense and get this over with. "We found it—"

"Yeah, I heard. Thanks."

She eyed him as he approached with that hips-first stride, so unlike an Amish man. "Are you feeling better?"

"Never better, now that you're here."

This was getting tiresome. "Sorry about your boots." The fancy boots wouldn't have reacted well to their sudden immersion in the water. "Can you get them treated?"

He shrugged. "I'll just order another pair. Maybe not the ostrich, though. If I'm going to film in them, I'll need something more practical, like a struggling rancher would have worn in 1942."

Ostrich boots! With an effort, Malena closed her mouth on the exclamation. Then she said, "Has your trainer arrived?"

"Not yet. It'll be a couple of days."

Trey put in, "But Grayson's back from his corporate retreat, so Cord is good to go."

"I'm glad to hear it. Cord, my father hopes someone can come get your bags this morning."

Instead of looking like he knew he was being booted out, he looked pleased at the prospect. "I'll give you a lift home and get them. Trey here let me borrow a toothbrush last night, but I think it might have been used." The two young men grinned.

With relief that he was being cooperative now that everything was going his way, she said. "I'll wait for you outside."

"Come and join us for breakfast," Trey said, waving in the direction of another wide hallway, this one illuminated by skylights and with deer and antelope trophy heads mounted on the walls.

But she shook her head. "I had mine two hours ago. But don't let me hold you up."

"Save me some," Cord told his host. He pulled his truck keys from his jeans pocket. "I'll be back soon."

"Take the long way home," Trey said with a laugh, and sauntered out.

There *was* no long way home. The two outfits shared a property line. Malena shook her head at herself—clearly it was some *Englisch* figure of speech.

The truck was parked in the guest lot between the house and a stable block nearly the same size. Cord opened the door for her, so as she climbed in, she made sure her skirts remained modest and tucked them around her before she fastened the seat belt. "Are you sure you're okay to drive?"

He chuckled. "You make it sound like I've been drinking already."

"You were pretty wobbly yesterday. Sara was worried. That's why she suggested the clinic."

"I'm fine." He backed the truck around and headed down

the driveway, which, unlike the Circle M's lane, was paved. At the gates, he stopped the vehicle and gazed at her expectantly.

She wasn't about to give him the satisfaction of turning the tables on her. She slid out to the running board and jumped to the ground. Why these big diesel pickups had to be so high you had to enter them in two steps, she would never understand. Chance Madison had told her once it was for better visibility, but she had a feeling it had more to do with being higher than your neighbors as you barrelled down the highway. She opened Alden's beautiful gates for him, waited for him to idle through, then closed them, dropping the bar carefully into place. Only when the highway was safe from escaping cattle did she rejoin him in the cab.

Their lane wasn't far, thank goodness. She wouldn't be trapped in this truck, as high in the air as a hay wagon, for long.

"So how was the big fish fry?" he asked. "What did I miss?"

"It was good. Even after everyone ate as much as they wanted, there were trout left over. We're going to make fish fritters for lunch today."

"Sounds fattening."

"Oh, it is," she said happily. "Battered and deep fried."

He made a face. "What did you do after supper? Hymns?"

"No, we played volleyball."

"That sounds wholesome. Who won?"

She glanced at him, driving with his right hand draped over the top of the wheel, his left elbow hanging out the open window. "We don't play to win. Nobody keeps score. We just play until everyone has had a chance to serve the ball a couple of times, and then we go in for dessert."

"Don't tell me. Apple cake. Because Alden was there."

Their lane flashed past on the right.

"No, we—Cord, you just passed our lane. You can turn around at the curve up there—there's room in front of the cattle gate."

He didn't even slow down. "Eventually."

Was that a smug smile on his face? What was he doing?

"Cord! I have plans this morning. Please turn around so you can get your things."

"What plans?"

"That's none of your business!"

"If you tell me, maybe I'll turn around."

"I'm not going to make silly bargains with you," she said furiously. But she didn't see a choice. She couldn't very well leap out of the cab at sixty miles an hour. Reluctantly, she said, "I'm going to town with my mother and Lovina."

"Think of the time you'll save. I'm going to take you to breakfast at the café. By the time we're done, your mom will just be trotting in."

"I don't want breakfast. I told you. I just ate."

"Well, I do. Come on, Malena. What does a guy have to do to spend a little time with you?"

Not take me where I don't want to go, maybe?

The truck ran over the yellow line and he jerked it back just in time to miss an oncoming pickup.

"Would you pay attention?" she cried.

"It's not my fault I have to resort to kidnapping to get you alone." He grinned as though he'd said something funny. "In fact, I just had an idea. How about we have breakfast in Libby? I hear there's a big Amish restaurant down there."

"They're not Amish," she snapped. "I'm not going to Libby, especially not with you. Stop the truck, please."

Something glinted in his eyes—those intense blue eyes that

could snap like lightning when his temper was up. Some people might have taken it for amusement. She knew better.

Behold, I send you forth as sheep in the midst of wolves: be ye therefore wise as serpents, and harmless as doves.

She wasn't very good at being a dove, but if she didn't try, she'd find herself forty miles away in Libby, completely at his mercy.

Mei Vater, hilfe mich.

"All right," she said in a softer tone, though it sounded to her more like resignation. "Maybe I am a little hungry. The Bitterroot Dutch Café has a really good egg and sausage pie you might like. More protein. Better for you than the chocolate pancakes with blueberry sauce."

"I wouldn't eat chocolate pancakes on a bet, with or without sauce. One plate probably has ten thousand calories."

"Probably," she agreed. She'd agree to anything as long as they stopped in Mountain Home. Once they were seated at the café, she'd pretend to go to the restroom and dive out the back door. She could make it to the safety of Alden's smithy in less than a minute.

Ahead, she could see a buggy approaching on the opposite side, heading out of town. They were too far away just yet to see whose it was, but good grief, all she needed was for someone to get a look at her riding in a truck at a breakneck speed with the movie star. Goodness knew what the Amish grapevine would do with *that*.

The truck drifted to the right, and she shot an alarmed glance at Cord. He was frowning. Blinking as though trying to focus.

"Are you all right?" She didn't have to pretend concern. Cold anxiety was pooling in her stomach.

"Yep. Why do you ask?"

"Well—" *Dove. Be a dove.* "I'm worried about you."

"Aw, say it isn't so."

He rubbed his eyes and the truck drifted to the left, over the double line.

Her stomach plunged. "Cord! Watch out!"

It was the Stolzfus girls!

He jerked the wheel over, then tried to straighten out. But they were going too fast.

Beth slapped the reins over her horse's back and, startled, it plunged ahead just in time for the truck to avoid the buggy itself. It struck the rear buggy lamp, destroying it in less than a second. Glass shattered and through Cord's open window, Malena heard a scream.

The big pickup plowed through the gravel on the shoulder, slewed as Cord lost control of the wheel, then something went *bang!* They plunged into the ditch. Flowers—the opposite bank —water—they all flew up at Malena's face. She slammed forward so hard she lost her breath.

Instinctively, she flung up her arms to shield her face from breaking glass. The seat belt stopped her from going through. Then a huge, hard object hit her and drowned out her scream of sheer terror.

17

THE CELLPHONE RANG in Alden's shop and he sighed. Just when he'd found a comfortable rhythm with the twisted bars he was stockpiling in case Doc MacDonald had been serious about that gate. He pulled off his gloves and headed for the desk, then wasted another ring trying to find the noisy thing under a pile of paperwork.

"Stolzfus Smith and Farrier. Alden sp—"

"Alden!" Julie shrieked. "Come quick! There's been an accident."

His stomach did a double flip and twisted itself into a knot. *"Bischt du okay?"*

"Ja, ja, we're fine, but … oh, Alden, a big truck hit us and it's in the ditch."

A sudden vision of an eighteen-wheeler filled with liquid nitrogen or something equally horrific filled his head. "How big? Get away from it!"

"A pickup—the one I saw before. Cord McLean's pickup. And Alden, there's a girl in there with him. An *Amish* girl. They're not moving. Please come, as fast as you can."

An Amish girl?

"Where are you?"

"I—I don't know. A little ways out. I can see the Zook brothers' house from here, and there's a great big clump of wild roses on the fence."

Mile marker two.

Without even saying good-bye, Alden clicked off the phone and called 9-1-1. He rapidly explained what had happened, and the dispatcher told him the EMTs were on the way. He had a second to wonder if Zach was on shift today before he forgot everything except grabbing up a couple of crowbars and wishing he'd had the sense to put together a first-aid kit long before this.

It was only by *Gott*'s grace that he'd brought some metal stock over to the shop with Joseph this morning. It would save him a flat-out run back to the house to get the horse. He had the big Belgian hitched up again in record time, and pushed him to his considerable limits for the two miles of highway.

Two miles had never taken so long in all his life.

As he rounded the curve, he recognized Cord McLean's truck, nose down in the ditch. On the far side, the sound of a siren shut off as the boxy EMT van rocked to a halt. Joseph headed straight for his stable mate, Timothy, and the buggy, which was pulled up a distance past both.

Julie had taken his frantic command to get away from the truck literally.

Broken amber glass sparkled on the shoulder of the road and crunched under his wheels, which were not rubberized. He pulled up and leaped from the farrier's wagon. "Julie? Beth? Are you all right?"

The girls were standing on the off side of the horse, and fell into his hug together. "We're okay. But we're so afraid," Beth said, her voice wobbling, on the edge of tears. "Alden, I think it's Malena."

His knees went weak. He took a deep breath that was more like a gasp.

"Pray," he croaked. Then he turned and jogged back toward the EMT van, whose lights were flashing in warning to the oncoming traffic.

Down in the ditch, one of the EMTs had the driver's side door open and was talking to the person inside. Cord.

But Alden's concern lay entirely on the other side.

Don't let it be Malena. But that was evil. It could be any of the *Youngie* and he had to help, no matter who it was.

He slid down the bank to find Zach Miller up to his ankles in water, hauling on the door for all it was worth. The truck was slightly tilted toward the passenger side, and part of the door and the truck bed were stove in. A motionless form leaned against the window, the seatbelt still fastened and the deployed airbag draped all over her.

Zach looked up, his face calm but desperation tugging at the corners of his eyes. "I can't get it open. I can't get to her."

"I've got crowbars."

Denki, Lieber Gott, for prompting me to grab them on the way.

In seconds, he was back with the crowbars. With Zach on the top and Alden on the base of the door, they heaved in unison.

The heavy door groaned open and Malena's limp form sagged out. Alden reached for her as though his entire soul would escape his body if he didn't.

"Don't touch her!" Zach commanded. "Her spine could be hurt. I've got a backboard right here. Once I get her secured on it, we'll lower her into the sled."

Dazed, Alden realized that Zach's medical equipment lay in the flowers, ready for use. He didn't know how Zach could be so calm as he worked with swift gentleness on his sister's unconscious form. Alden, who was not a crier, was barely keeping the tears at bay, and had to wipe his eyes with his sleeve to see clearly.

At last Malena was secured in the sled, and together, they carried her up the slope to the van. Traffic was creeping by, people staring out their windows wide-eyed. And there was the youngest Madison boy in his truck, gawking into the back of the van, where Cord was already strapped into a cot for transport to the clinic.

He didn't know what had possessed her to get into the truck of such a reckless driver. There was only one reason he could think of—that secretly, she must somehow be attracted to him. That after the scare in the river, she had realized which of them she really cared for, and grabbed the chance to be alone with him.

That she was baptized into the Amish church, that he was as worldly as a man could get—none of this would have mattered, maybe, when her heart was involved. If there was anything he knew about Malena, it was that when her heart was in something, it was in it the whole way, come what may.

Someone was calling his name.

"Alden!" Zach shook his arm. "Are you OK? You look like you're in shock."

He blinked, and the images shattered into pieces in his mind.

And fell into his heart, like shards of glass.

"It looks like the truck sideswiped the telephone pole after it brushed your sisters' buggy. You need to get them home.

And call the Circle M. Tell them what happened. Mamm will want to drive to the clinic right away."

"*Ja*. Right away."

Zach leaped into the back of the van with his two patients, the other EMT slammed the doors, and in a moment they had wheeled into the eastbound lane toward Mountain Home, siren wailing and lights flashing.

Alden was never going to be able to hear that sound in future and not think of this moment.

He found his sisters waiting by the buggy, which was somehow not damaged except for the buggy lamp on the rear. "Can you drive?" he asked Beth.

When she shook her head, still clearly shaken and pale, Julie put an arm around her. "I can. Will you follow us?"

"*Ja*. Turn around. By then I'll have collected my crowbars and maybe this traffic will have cleared."

The Madison boy's truck was gone, so presumably the Rocking Diamond had already heard what had happened to their accident-prone guest. There was nothing to be done about the truck—its passenger door wasn't about to close anytime soon. With any luck, the Madison boys would return and pull it out of the ditch a second time. He wasn't about to hitch Joseph to it and pull it out, though he was pretty sure the big horse could do it.

That wasn't his job. His job was to see his sisters safely home.

And call the Circle M.

And somehow find the words to tell them what had happened.

200

Naomi was in the habit of keeping the cellphone in the cookie jar. Cookies never lasted long enough around the ranch to actually make it into the jar, but it was a *gut* place to keep the phone—out of sight, out of mind.

On the rare occasions when it did ring, it vibrated inside the china container, sounding like the big, old-fashioned alarm clock with two bells that Malena had to use. The racket was the only thing that woke her up.

Naomi fished the noisy thing out and pressed the talk button. "Circle M Ranch."

"Naomi, this is Alden Stolzfus. Zach told me to call."

Zach was on shift at the volunteer fire department. There was only one reason he would have told someone else to call and not used his own work phone: he was in the van looking after an injured person.

Her skin chilled from head to foot. The only member of her family who was unaccounted for was Malena.

In the background on his end, she could hear the rapid clip-clop of big hoofs. A car going past. Things rattling. Metal things.

Alden was in his farrier's wagon, and Zach had told him to phone.

A cold trickle of dread seeped into her stomach. "What has happened, Alden?" She tried to keep her voice steady. "Is it Malena?"

"*Ja*. She was riding in the pickup with Cord and it ran off the road after knocking the buggy lamp off my sisters' buggy. I'm following them into town now."

The picture in her mind was no less vivid for being described in so few words. "And Zach?"

"He's gone in the EMT van with her and Cord. He told me to phone. That you'd want to go to the clinic."

She forced herself to breathe. "How bad is it, Alden? Did you see her?"

He swallowed, and even with all the noise, she could hear it. "I don't know. She wasn't awake. We had to pry the door open with a crowbar—it hit a telephone pole before it went into the ditch."

Naomi's knees quit working and she sat at the kitchen table so suddenly the salt shaker fell over. "But she's alive?"

"*Ja.* The airbag went off. Maybe it knocked her out. I don't know. Anyway, Zach is with her."

"*Denki* for telling me, Alden. You'll be with her, too."

There was a long silence. "I don't think so. Zach said only you. And probably Reuben. Family."

"But—"

"I have to see to my sisters. I—I hope she'll be all right."

And he disconnected.

Naomi stared at the phone in her hand as the call light went out. What did he mean, *I don't think so?*

The man she had seen last night had revolved around Malena the way the earth revolved around the sun. The way the church revolved around *der Herr.* That man would have seen to his family and then nothing would have prevented him from meeting her and Reuben at the clinic. Nothing.

Sara and Rebecca, she realized suddenly, were in the kitchen doorway, each with a baby on her hip and identical expressions of fear in their eyes.

Rapidly, she told them what had happened. She pulled on her away bonnet, grabbed her handbag from the dresser, and ran down the steps.

Reuben, thank merciful Heaven, was in the barn, just hitching up Hester for a trip to town that had an entirely different purpose now.

She had barely gabbled out what had happened when she found herself in his strong arms. "Breathe, *Liewi*. Take a moment. Take a breath. We will pray."

She obeyed, her chest rising and falling against his as she appealed to their heavenly Father for His help. When she opened her eyes, the sight of the track a tear had made down her husband's cheek nearly broke her. "Our Malena!" she said on a sob.

"Our Zachariah is with her," Reuben said hoarsely. "He'll do everything in his power for his *Schweschder*. I'll finish hitching up and we'll go. The girls will tell Lovina what happened."

Somehow nothing was as bad when she and Reuben faced it together. Not even the sight of that foolish truck, face down in the ditch like a broken bird, one door hanging open. The passenger door. Where Malena had been sitting.

She choked back a cry of dismay and hid her face in Reuben's shoulder until they were long past the sight.

The private neurological rehabilitation clinic on the far side of town did not only cater to those recovering from trauma. Not for the first time, Naomi breathed a prayer of thanks that one of its doctors rotated in from the county hospital in Libby to staff a small emergency department. Instead of going to the rehabilitation wing, as they had done to find Rebecca and the man who had believed himself engaged to her last spring, they went to the busy ER at the back.

The woman at the desk made a phone call, and in a moment Zach came through the swinging doors. "Mamm. Dat. Back here."

"Is she—" Reuben's voice choked into silence.

"She's awake. She's talking," Zach said.

Naomi's breath whooshed out of her and she would have burst into tears in the privacy of her away bonnet, except she needed to be calm for Reuben's sake. He loved his twin girls to pieces, and even a skinned knee or a bump on the head from a fall would upset him badly until he could take the little hurt to *der Herr* for comfort.

They found Malena in one of a series of curtained-off cubicles that lined a long room. With Reuben and Zach right behind her, Naomi slipped inside to see her vibrant, laughing girl still and pale against the white sheets. Even her hair seemed to have lost some of its intensity. Her *Kapp* lay on a narrow table at the foot of the bed.

She had no prayer covering. And her hair had been taken down.

"Mamm." Malena held up her arms the way she had as a baby, asking to be picked up.

Naomi folded her into the gentlest hug of which she was capable, considering she wanted to crush her girl against her chest and never let her go. She stood aside so that Reuben could do the same. Then they sank into the plastic chairs Zach had produced, and Naomi had time to look her over.

A black eye.

A big bruise on one forearm, as though she had fended off an attack.

A splint on the third finger of her left hand.

"It looks worse than it is," Zach said hastily, seeing what little color remaining in Naomi's face draining out of it. "The bruises are from the air bag deploying, and she sprained her finger."

"It could be worse, but it doesn't feel like it," Malena offered, her voice weak.

"I'm glad it isn't worse," Reuben said, his voice hoarse with emotion. "How did you come to be in that truck, *Dochsder*?"

"He was supposed to drive me home and get his luggage.

But he wanted breakfast at the café. I tried to make him stop. He wouldn't listen."

Reuben's face went motionless. Naomi knew her husband was holding back words meant for Cord McLean, not his defenseless daughter. She was holding back quite a few, too.

"From what she's told me, I think that knock on the head in the river the other night might have resulted in something else wrong with him," Zach said. "Something the doctor on duty that night might have missed."

"At least he's in the right place to find out," Naomi managed. "We'll pray for him."

After a moment, Reuben nodded in agreement.

"How long will they keep her?" she asked her capable son.

"Honestly, she came out of it pretty well. I'll go out and check, but I'm sure you can take her home with you today."

Joy and relief welled up in Naomi like water in a spring, and she squeezed Reuben's hand.

"I have to get back to work," Zach said, leaning down to give her a squeeze around the shoulders. "See you all at home. I'm off at two."

It took a while, between the release paperwork and waiting at the pharmacy for medicine, but at length Malena climbed carefully into the buggy. Instead of taking her place next to Reuben, Naomi sat on the rear bench beside her with one arm around her.

"Oh, Mamm," her daughter sighed, cuddling closer. "I was so afraid."

"It's over now, *Liewi*."

Reuben shook the reins over Hester's back, and they started up the clinic's long, winding drive with its unseasonably plush green lawns on either side.

"*Gott* was with you," Naomi continued softly, marveling at

yet more evidence that He held them all in the hollow of his hand. "His grace was sufficient for you. I hope you'll find it in your heart to forgive that poor young man. Was he badly hurt?"

"I don't know. He went one way and I went the other. He probably has bruises like mine, though."

A throbbing sound seemed to surround them, and Hester tossed her head and looked askance at the helicopter with the big red cross painted on it. It settled onto a circular concrete pad close to the side doors of the clinic. Some other poor soul was experiencing the worst day of their life, too, it seemed. Naomi hoped it would have as positive an ending as their own.

As they rounded the last curve, a big Belgian pulling a heavy wagon clattered into view, going fast enough that its driver had to haul on the reins to get it to stop.

"Reuben?" The wagon drew even with them. "Do you have news of Malena?"

"Better than that, I have my girl right here," Reuben said, tilting his head toward the two of them in the back. "They've just released her. We're taking her home."

"Stand, Joseph." There was a jingle of harness as Joseph shook his mane, and a thump of boots. Alden Stolzfus slid aside the passenger door and peered in, for there were, of course, no windows in the back. "Malena? Are you all right?"

"*Ja,*" Malena told him, her voice warm even if it was a little woozy from the medicine. "I'm okay."

"Bruises and a sprained finger. No more, thanks be to *Gott,*" Naomi said.

"Pray for Cord," Malena said dreamily. "I don't think he came out so well."

Alden's face looked stricken, and he backed away as though he had been slapped. "I will," was all he said.

And then Reuben was urging Hester on. Naomi turned to look out the back window. Alden was standing at his horse's shoulder, gazing after them as though it had suddenly turned into the worst day of his life, too.

18

Three days later

EVERYONE AT CHURCH in the Zook barn loft on Sunday had already heard what had happened—all it took was one buggy passing the accident scene, and by supper time that night, news of the accident had been all over the valley.

In a way, Malena thought, it was a relief. For one, she didn't have to repeat the story twenty times. And for another, while people might stare at the spectacular bruise on her face, it was with sympathy, and always with the wish that they could do something for her. One of the Zook brothers had gruffly offered a little jar of homemade arnica cream, and so far it had provided the most relief. She didn't like to take the pain medicine the doctor had ordered; she didn't need it except if someone bumped one of the bruises, and besides, it made her woozy. So the arnica cream had been very welcome.

After the fellowship meal of macaroni and cheese, whipped peanut butter sandwiches, and salad and pickles from the Zook garden, which seemed to grow fatter, redder tomatoes than anyone else's, the *Youngie* congregated outside. The sun was warm, though each day its arc through the sky was a little more shallow. Roundup was on Labor Day weekend, and after that the snow could fly at any time.

Malena talked and did her best to laugh without moving her face too much. And all the while she wondered why she didn't catch more than a passing glimpse of Alden. If she was in the front yard, he was over by the horses with some of the other young men. If she was in the house, he was in the barn. The difference between today and the night of the fishing frolic couldn't be more marked, and she couldn't figure out why. Even a discreet inquiry of Julie netted her nothing. Julie had seen nothing unusual about her brother's behavior. All she'd said was that he'd been pretty shaken up by helping to extract Malena from the truck.

Malena had no memory of it. Which was a shame. Even through her pain and fear, she would have appreciated being rescued by Alden. And even with the bruises now, it would have been a sight better than being ignored by him.

By suppertime, when most of the families had gone home and only the *Youngie* remained for the singing, it was glaringly obvious that something had gone very wrong between them. As Connie Zook, one of the visiting nieces of their hosts, announced the first hymn, Malena made up her mind.

Unwomanly it might be. Forward it definitely would be. But Alden Stolzfus was not going home alone.

Mind you, if he asked to take another girl home, Malena would probably just die of hurt and shame right there on the spot.

But she couldn't think about that. She needed to figure out how she was going to pull this off without making a spectacle of herself in front of everyone and frightening Alden away permanently.

Wouldn't her twin laugh at the very thought of Malena doing her best to be quiet and discreet! But that wonderful feeling of being together with Alden even when they sat at opposite ends of the room? It was gone. With every fiber of her being, Malena wanted it back. She needed to know *why* it had gone, and she was prepared to do whatever it took to erase this distance between them.

A glow behind the peaks of the mountains told her the full moon was about to rise and pour its silver light into the valley. She made her way across the Zook side yard as though she planned to collect a horse. Since she'd expected to go home with Alden, she'd come with Rebecca and Zach as usual, and Zach would come for Hester whenever he got going. The shadows beside Alden's buggy were as black as Timothy's glossy coat. The grass brushed her ankles, releasing its sweet scent, and against the fence a clump of wild roses had already begun to turn to hips. The air was soft with the moisture in the night air—they might get a little rain tonight.

Footsteps passed the buggy on the other side, and she moved farther into its shadow. She would recognize those shoulders and the shape of his head anywhere. Alden whistled up the horse, which trotted over and met him at the gate. She didn't move as he backed Timothy between the slats, hardly breathed when he came over to her side of the animal to finish fastening the buckles. Just as he climbed in, that's when she'd make her move and—

"Can I give you a ride home, Malena?"

Surprise tingled through her like a jolt of static electricity. So much for stealth. "How did you know I was here?"

"Your shampoo. It smells like strawberries."

Her insides went all soft and gooey. That had to be a good sign. "*Ja*, I would like a ride home. If—if you don't have other plans."

"*Neh*. No other plans."

Silently, they both climbed into the buggy, and Alden backed it into the drive. In minutes they were rolling away, the Yoder boys razzing them for all they were worth as they caught a glimpse of a *Maedsche's* white *Kapp* in its depths. It could have been any *Maedsche* and the teasing would have been the same. She was just glad that it was her and not someone else.

"Alden, what's wrong?"

"Nothing. I was happy you were well enough to come to church today."

"You don't seem very happy. You've avoided me all day. Did I do something wrong?"

He was silent.

Malena was not about to allow silence. "I haven't seen you since I came home from the clinic, so it can't be any of the mistakes I made on Friday or Saturday. And everything was wonderful between us on Wednesday, after the fishing frolic. So something happened on Thursday. Besides the accident. What was it? Please tell me."

He made a soft sound that might have been a chuckle. "You sound like a detective. Or my mother when she's tracking down who ate the berries she was saving for dessert."

Malena waited. He was stalling. Finally, she said softly, "I don't like this distance between us. Plain speaking, remember?"

After a moment, he nodded. "Anyplace you particularly like? I was thinking we might take a moonlight walk."

As though the moon had been waiting for its cue, it slid into the space between two peaks and suddenly the road became a ribbon of silver, drawn taut until it reached the belt of trees that concealed the bishop's house.

"Turn in to the Circle M. We can walk up to where Adam's house is going to be. It's one of my favorite spots."

Ten minutes later they were walking through the deep meadow grass dotted with flowers, some with their blossoms closed for the night. The moonlight was nearly as good as broad daylight. She led him up to a flat rock where Adam sometimes sat, giving him a view of the whole clearing that would one day hold a house.

They seated themselves side by side. She thought he might take her hand, but he laid them on either side of his thighs, his feet dangling down. It was only about six inches between his boots and the ground, but they'd discovered as children this rock made a *gut* seat. And it was particularly good for talking things over.

"Is there ... anything between you and Cord McLean?" Alden's voice was gruff, and he spoke to the meadow, not directly to her.

Astonishment stole all the words from her tongue.

He seemed to sense that she was staring at him, stupefied, and glanced at her, almost as though he was ashamed for asking.

"Neh," she finally managed to say. "What would make you think that?"

"Because ... you were riding with him."

"Not willingly. At least, not after he passed the Circle M and refused to turn around. Not after he threatened to take me to Libby. Not after—"

"He was going to take you to *Libby?*" She'd really shocked him now.

"I had to agree to have breakfast with him in Mountain

Home, or he'd have driven me down there and goodness knows what would have happened. And do you know what?"

"I'm afraid to ask."

"As soon as we got to the café, I was going to run out the back and over to the smithy. All I could think of was how fast I could get to you, Alden. Because I knew I would be safe with you. And the next thing I knew—"

She gasped to a halt with the memory of the bank rushing up at her—the painful blow of the air bag—the awful crunch of what she'd learned afterward had been a telephone pole. And worst of all, the scream of the girls in the buggy—

Her eyes filled with tears. "I was so glad to learn that Julie and Beth were safe. I don't know what I would have done if I'd been a part of—of hurting them."

He took her cold hand in his warm one, and something inside her came undone. She went into his arms and he held her while she cried it all out. The fear. The pain. The shame of having gone anywhere with a worldly man. The relief that she and Alden were talking again.

Some of it she managed to say. And for a wonder, he seemed to understand more than the jerky, tear-soaked words conveyed.

When at last she lifted her head, she saw another wonder. His lean cheeks were streaked with tears, too.

"I thought for one terrible moment that you were dead," he choked out against her hair. "And I knew. Right then, I knew."

She waited, holding him tightly, the unbruised side of her face against his collarbone. In the silence, she could feel his heart thumping as though he had run five miles to be with her. He had promised her plain speaking, and he would keep his promise.

He drew a shuddering breath. "I knew that if *Gott* had seen fit to take you, then I would be like the Zook brothers, and spend the rest of my life alone."

She could hardly believe he meant such a thing. "*Ach, neh*, Alden. You were meant to be a husband, a father. To teach *Kinner* how to love *der Herr*, and to make a loving home for your *Fraa*. Being unmarried would be wrong for you."

"It would be more wrong to marry someone else knowing that my heart belonged to you. It always has, Malena. Since the first time I walked into your house for church and saw you sitting in a sunbeam, your hair glowing like fire and your face ..." He stopped, and she felt his body temperature rise, as though he were blushing.

"My poor face," she whispered. "It's a fine shade of purple today. Mamm promises it will be a lovely yellow tomorrow."

"Bruised or not, it's beautiful to me. When Zach told me you were breathing, it was all I could do not to fall to my knees in that ditch and praise *Gott*."

"I feel like praising Him right now." And safe in the circle of his arms, she did, in a silent prayer of joy. She stole a glance at him, and saw his face raised to the stars, as if he were doing the same.

After a moment, he came back to earth. "It's too soon to ask you the question I want to ask you," he said, "but I want you to know that I'm going to. Maybe not this month. Or this year. But someday soon, I'm going to."

The last of the knot inside her, the one that told her she was too much, too loud, too everything, unravelled. She wasn't too much for Alden. She knew now that she was completely enough.

And maybe some days, *too everything* wasn't a bad thing at all.

She lifted her lashes to find his gaze on her. Those eyes, shadowed now, but glittering when the moonlight found them. That mouth, smiling. And that dimple, which now she had every right to touch.

So she did. "And I want you to know that someday soon, I'll probably say yes."

"Plain speaking?"

"Mm?"

"I'm going to kiss you. Not someday soon. Now."

"Oh, I hope so." That was her, the most forward Amish girl in the valley.

He chuckled. "Plain speaking. I love it. But not the way I love you."

"And I you," she said softly, body and soul thrilling with the wonder of it.

And when his mouth found hers, so sweet and yet so full of the wonder of discovery, she learned that there were some occasions when a kiss could speak more plainly and reveal much more than words ever could.

*

THE WESTERN NEWS
August 26

ACTOR'S ACCIDENT LEADS TO STARTLING DISCOVERY

Libby, MT—On Thursday, August 19, actor Cord McLean met with a mishap that nearly took his life and that of an unnamed companion. McLean has been staying at the Rocking Diamond Ranch, learning ranch management and cowboying in preparation for his next movie. *Ride Forever* is expected to be one of the biggest summer releases of next year, and possibly in the running for the actor's first Academy Award.

McLean was driving on the county highway when he lost control of his vehicle, sideswiped a passing Amish buggy, collided with a telephone pole, and wound up in one of the deep ditches in common use in Lincoln County. He was taken by the local EMTs to a medical clinic close by.

"There," says Mrs Taylor Madison, a generous donor to the clinic, "he was life-flighted to the hospital in Missoula." During the course of his examination, among other non-life-threatening injuries, the doctors found that the actor had an undiagnosed cataract in his left eye. Surgery was performed immediately and readers can be assured that he is expected to make a full recovery.

"We had seen odd signs that possibly his vision was compromised, but we never suspected anything like this in someone so young. Mr McLean has asked me to thank all his fans for their support," Mrs Madison said with a grateful smile. "He should be back in the saddle as soon as the doctors give their approval."

This publication hopes he will heal quickly and well, and wishes him every success in his film career.

EPILOGUE
THE CIRCLE M RANCH

October 12

IF ANYONE HAD TOLD Zach Miller a year ago that his youngest brother Joshua would be dressed in new clothes and getting married while already the father of a child, he would have thought that person was *narrisch*. But such a person wasn't in the congregation that morning. Zach was. Right up at the front next to his brother. And he could see the love in Joshua's eyes as he gazed at his bride sitting opposite him in her blue dress and white organdy cape and apron.

Sara, the former disgrace and fence-jumper.

Joshua, the black sheep of the Miller family.

Frankly, it was a miracle sent from *Gott* that these two should have found each other and that His love and theirs could do such a work of transformation.

Their brother Daniel sat with his and Lovina's son Joel on the men's side, both their faces solemn. Zach and his brother Adam were acting as *Neuwesitzern*. They sat opposite Malena and Rebecca, who were supporting Sara in the absence of the family she'd been born into and whom *Gott* had gathered to Himself years ago. Behind them, on the women's side, were their parents and Lovina, holding their baby sister Deborah and Joshua's son Nathan. Kate Weaver sat with the single women farther back.

Single for not much longer. For as Malena had predicted, Adam and Kate had come back engaged after their summer in Whinburg Township. They weren't wasting any time, either. Their wedding was to be the first week in December, and the whole family was going back to Pennsylvania for it, and staying with Dat's cousins Melvin and Carrie Miller just outside the town of Whinburg. Family on both sides were coming from all over—Indiana, other counties in Pennsylvania, even Prince Edward Island in maritime Canada, where Kate's aunt and uncle and her cousins had settled.

What a year it had been. When love came to the Circle M, it arrived in no uncertain terms. First Daniel and Lovina, then Joshua and Sara so unexpectedly. Neither of his sisters had predictable, ordinary courtships, either. He and Noah King had got to talking one day after roundup while they were out repairing the Kings' old barn, and Noah had confided that he meant to propose to Becca soon.

Maybe even tonight, after supper.

Zach had no doubt at all that Noah would have wangled it so that Sara paired him with Rebecca. Likewise Malena and Alden. Couples who were openly dating usually sat together, but Rebecca was the kind who liked to be certain.

As certain as she was that Noah was the man she wanted to spend the rest of her life with.

As certain as Malena was that Alden was the choice *Gott* had made for her.

The thought of *Gott*'s work in his brothers and sisters gave

Zach a bone-deep joy ... but floating on the surface like a piece of driftwood was the question that had been plaguing him for months now.

Why not me, Lord? When are You going to show me the woman You mean for me?

But *der Herr* had other work to do today that didn't include soothing Zach's aching heart.

The preacher's sermon on the faithful couples of the Old Testament came to a close. Isaac and Rebecca, Jacob and Rachel—couples as familiar to them all as any in the *Gmee*. The *Vorsinger* began the fourth verse of *Lied* 69, which in the Mountain Home community always came just before the vows began.

Er hat ein Weib genommen,
Die Christlich Kirch im Geist,
Die Liebe hat ihn drungen,
Die er uns auch hat g'leist.
Sein Leben hat er vor uns g'stellt,
Die ihm auch also lieben
Sind ihm auch auserwahlt.

He has taken a wife
The Christian Church in the Spirit,
The love that so compelled him
He also gave to us.
Before us he's laid his life,
So those who likewise love him
Are also chosen for him.

As their voices died away, Little Joe Wengerd, looking as solemn as the occasion required, rose to his feet. Zach shifted in his chair and sat up straighter.

"Here before me come a man and a woman who have agreed to enter the state of matrimony—Sara Fischer and Joshua Miller. If any here has an objection to the marriage, he now has opportunity to make it known." In the silence of the Miller living room, a baby gurgled. Some of the *Youngie* chuckled, quickly silenced. The bishop's clear blue eyes twinkled as returned his gaze to the couple. "No one but your son appears to have an opinion, so if you are still minded the same, you may now come forth in the name of the Lord."

Looking abashed at Nathan's contribution to their ceremony, Sara and Joshua stood to take their places in front of the bishop, places that only a few months ago Daniel and Lovina had occupied. In a few months from now, it might be Adam and Kate. Once again Zach marveled at the power of *Gott* to accomplish so much in so short a time.

Little Joe turned his gaze on Joshua. The twinkle dimmed with the solemnity of the moment, but didn't leave his eyes.

"Can you confess, Brother, that you accept this our sister as your wife, and that you will not leave her until death separates you?" he asked. "And do you believe that this is from the Lord and that you have come so far by faith and prayer?"

"I do," Joshua said, a hitch in his voice.

Truer words, Zach thought, had never been spoken.

"And you, Sister—do you confess that you accept this our brother as your husband, and that you will not leave him until death separates you? And do you believe that this is from the Lord and that you have come so far by faith and prayer?"

"I do," Sara said in a soft but clear voice that Zach was sure they could hear all the way to the back.

First Josh, then Sara vowed to be loyal to the other, to care for the other in sickness and adversity, in weakness and in moments when life was hard and they lost their courage.

Then Little Joe took their right hands between both of his sinewy rancher's paws, and announced in his booming voice, "The God of Abraham, the God of Isaac, and the God of Jacob be with you together and give His rich blessing upon you and be merciful to you. I wish you the blessings of God for a good beginning and a steadfast middle and a faithful ending, in and through the name of Jesus Christ. Amen." At the mention of the holy name of Christ, he and the bridal couple briefly bent their knees in respect. "Go forth in the name of the Lord," he said happily. This was clearly his favorite part. "You are now man and wife."

The *Vorsinger* launched into number 712, *"Gelobt Sei Gott im höchsten Thron,"* the bridal hymn the *Gmee* always sang as the wedding party processed down the aisle and out the door. Sara dabbed tears of happiness from her face with a handkerchief Lovina had lovingly embroidered just for this moment, her other hand safe in that of Joshua.

As the bridal couple received the good wishes of the *Gmee* out on the deck, the living room was quickly transformed into a dining room, with tables and benches, and tablecloths and napkins in Sara's colors—eggshell blue and butter yellow. Zach and Adam, Rebecca and Malena sat with the bridal couple in the corner table called the *Eck*, which had been decorated with Mamm's best china and a pair of wedding cakes, all waiting for them when they came in.

Mamm and Dat carried on the wedding lunch traditions many enjoyed back East—celery, chicken roast, mashed potatoes, and so many cakes and desserts that Zach lost count. Merriment and visiting were the order of the day as Josh and

Sara moved from table to table, thanking their relatives and guests for coming, and handing out favors—the little hay dollies Sara had been making for weeks, to signify hope for the prosperity of their neighbors' herds and their own hay farm. They would be moving in as husband and wife tonight, now that the house was renovated and waiting for them.

Zach was the kind of person who needed a little quiet time periodically when there were a lot of people around. So it wasn't long before he slid out the back door and walked quickly up the hill path to Grossmammi's orchard.

For a miracle, he found it empty. He half expected one of his siblings to be taking a quiet moment here with the one they loved, but apparently they were having too much fun. He couldn't stay long—they planned to do a little singing for Joshua and Sara as people took their leave.

He leaned on an apple trunk and breathed deeply of the scent of the fruit.

"They'll be ready to pick any day now," came a soft voice. Ruby Wengerd stepped out from behind a particularly leafy Pippin. Her smile turned to a look of concern. "Sorry, did I startle you?"

"I didn't think anyone was here."

"That's why I'm here. But I can go." She took two steps toward the mouth of the box canyon.

"*Neh, neh, ischt okay.* I just came to get a little peace and quiet."

"So did I." She took a deep breath. "It smells so good in here. And it always seems a little warmer than anywhere else."

"That's why my great-grandmother planted the apple trees here. There's a natural spring, and it's sheltered. Everyone else thought she was *narrisch*, but she knew her apples."

Ruby grinned, then ducked her head as though to hide it.

"She knew she was right, and she went ahead and did it anyway, despite what people thought."

"*Ja*, that was Grossmammi." He took another breath as though it might fortify him. "Guess I'd better go back. They'll be singing soon, now that our parents have had their turn in the *Eck*, and someone will notice one of the *Neuwesitzern* is missing. Coming?"

"I think I'll stay another minute. I like the quiet."

He nodded, and ambled down the short lane between the rows of trees. His mind was already questing ahead. Who had Sara paired him with? Would she be the one *Gott* had set aside for him?

Would he ever find out, as wedding after wedding passed him by?

Questions without answers. But asking them took him out of the canyon and back to the bustle and joy of the day.

❧

RUBY WENGERD MOVED FROM UNDER THE WAVERING shadows of the leaves and into the sunlight to watch him go. Her fingers pressed against her lips as though to stop herself from calling out.

Why doesn't he see me, Lord? Zach Miller is the man I've loved for most of my life.

When is he going to realize that the woman You mean for him has always been right next door?

THE END

AFTERWORD
A NOTE FROM ADINA

I hope you've enjoyed the fifth book about the Miller family. If you subscribe to my newsletter, you'll hear about new releases in the series, my research in Montana, and snippets about quilting and writing and chickens—my favorite subjects!

I hope you'll join me by subscribing here:

https://www.subscribepage.com/shelley-adina

If you turn the page, you'll find a glossary of the Pennsylvania Dutch words used in this book. And now, here's a sneak peek at the final book in The Amish Cowboys of Montana series!

THE AMISH COWBOY'S HOME © ADINA SENFT

Home is where God's heart is. —Mountain Home Amish proverb

All her life, Ruby Wengerd has felt the eyes of the two Mountain Home Amish churches on her. Because she's the bishop's daughter, there's an unspoken expectation that she'll set the example for the *Youngie*. Watch her tongue and never give offense. And now that she's turned twenty, choose one of the valley's young men pursuing her and make a godly home.

But she doesn't want to make a home with anyone but Zach Miller. She's loved him for as long as she can remember —and he only sees her as a friend.

Zach has watched his brothers and sisters fall in love while he comes no closer to finding the one God means for him. At this rate, his infant sister will grow up and get married before he does. But at a Christmas wedding on the ranch, a stunning realization makes the scales fall from his eyes. It's as if he's seeing Ruby, his childhood friend, for the very first time. As the woman he's been waiting for. As his heart's home.

But Ruby may already have given up on him. The Amish grapevine is abuzz with speculation that she has been swept off her feet by a man from away and might even leave the valley. Is Zach really too late to court the girl next door?

The Montana Millers. They believe in faith, family, and the land. They'll need all three when love comes to the Circle M!

GLOSSARY

Spelling and definitions from Eugene S. Stine, *Pennsylvania German Dictionary* (Birdboro, PA: Pennsylvania German Society, 1996).

Words used:

Aendi: auntie

Ausbund: the Amish hymnal

bidde: please

Bischt du okay? Are you okay?

Bruder, Brieder: brother, brothers

Boppli(n): baby, babies

deemiedich: humble

Deitsch: Pennsylvania Dutch

denki: thank you

Der Herr: the Lord

Duchly: headscarf

Englisch: English language or English speakers

Freierei: courtship

Gmee: congregation

Gott: God

Gott's wille: God's will

gut: good

guder mariye: good morning

guder nacht: good night

hallich Geburtsdaag: happy birthday

hoch Dietsch: high German

hochmut: proud

Alles ischt okay? Is everything okay?

ja: yes

Kaffee: coffee

Kapp: prayer covering

Kinner: children

lieber Gott: dear God

Lied: song

Liewi: love, sweetie

Maedsche(r): girl(s)

Mann: man

mei Fraa: my wife

mei Freind: my friend

mei Soh: my son

Mei Vater, hilfe mich. My father, help me.

Millich: milk

narrisch: crazy

neh: no

Neuwesitzern: side-sitters; the bridal couple's supporters

Ordnung: discipline, or standard of behavior and dress unique to each community

Schweschder(e): sister(s)

Schwei: sister-in-law

verhuddelt: mixed up

Youngie: young people

&.

Amish Kindred Spirits

Emily of New Moon Quilts

Anna of the Island Bakery

Janelle of Lantern Point

Lizzie of Blue Castle Books

Clara of Windy Pines

*

Smoke River

Grounds to Believe

Pocketful of Pearls

The Sound of Your Voice

Over Her Head

*

Glory Prep (faith-based young adult)

Glory Prep

The Fruit of My Lipstick

Be Strong and Curvaceous

Who Made You a Princess?

Tidings of Great Boys

The Chic Shall Inherit the Earth

ABOUT THE AUTHOR

USA Today bestselling author Adina Senft grew up in a plain house church, where she was often asked by outsiders if she was Amish (the answer was no). She holds a PhD in Creative Writing from Lancaster University in the UK. Adina was the winner of RWA's RITA Award for Best Inspirational Novel in 2005, a finalist for that award in 2006, and was a Christy Award finalist in 2009. She appeared in the 2016 documentary film *Love Between the Covers*, is a popular speaker and convention panelist, and has been a guest on many podcasts, including Worldshapers and Realm of Books.

She writes steampunk adventure and mystery as Shelley Adina; and as Charlotte Henry, writes classic Regency romance. When she's not writing, Adina is usually quilting, sewing historical costumes, or enjoying the garden with her flock of rescued chickens.

Adina loves to talk with readers about books, quilting, and chickens!
www.adinasenft.com
adinasenft@comcast.net

Made in United States
North Haven, CT
05 April 2024

50939331R00145